Loves Cats, Anonymous

Loves Cats Series

Miranda Herald

My Koala Pouch

Cover design by Miblart

Contents

Also By Miranda Herald

Loves Cats Series:

Prequel Chapters: Willa's Blooper Reel- FREE at https://dl.bookfunnel.com/yqs4i2iqr0

Book 1: Loves Cats, Anonymous

Book 2: Swipe Right for More Cats

Puzzling through Romance Series:

Prequel Novella: Blundering through Paradise- FREE at https://dl.bookfunnel.com/q22azd8n2k

Book 1: Outwitting Paradise

Book 2: Misplacing Paradise

Book 3: Hiding Paradise

Book 4: Delivering Paradise

Smitten Scientists:

Catch and Release

Love, Lies and Investigations:

Security Breach of the Heart

Briarhaven Chronicles

Practical Guide Series:

Practical Guide to Magical Farming

Direwolf Series:

A Wolf in Sheep's Clothing

Chapter One

Show Dogs

When cats fly!

A fat, one-eyed calico cat went flying straight for Katrina's face. Wide-eyed and holding up her hands, she tried to catch it, but upon contact, instead of settling down, the cat clawed at her and tried to climb her red hair to get higher. In the background, she heard barking and hissing.

Who let a dog out?

A very wet, large black-lab mix rounded the corner, claws scampering on the linoleum. He shook himself, throwing water all over Katrina. At the sight of him, the cat scratched her while bounding out of her arms, hiding behind a pile of pet crates. She arched her back, hissing and spitting as the dog tried to get to her. Katrina tried to grab for the dog as he lunged into the crates, but the cat took off again and the dog after her. Katrina chased after them and heard the shake of a bag of treats as someone gave a sharp whistle. Distracted from the cat, the dog took off to another part of the shelter.

"Here, kitty, kitty, kitty..." Before long, Katrina spotted the one-eyed cat hiding on top of one of the cages. At first, the cat hissed as she approached, but Katrina's familiar presence and soft voice seemed to calm her. "Shhh, it's all right. The big bad dog is gone. You know, the vet is going to need to look you over again after jumping all over the room in your condition, sweetie pie. How did you get out here in the first place? You must be very clever to get loose."

With the cat safely secured in her arms, Katrina rounded the corner of Pet Friends Animal Shelter to see her best friend, Patrick, clipping a leash onto the particularly large and energetic dog. It was still soaking wet and jumping all over one of Katrina's new volunteers that was holding a bag of treats. Katrina looked over the small woman with the pixie haircut who just started today and racked her mind trying to remember her name... *Tara*.

After getting his charge under control, Patrick wiped his wet hand through his short black hair, making it stick down awkwardly. The dog whined and wiggled his tail as Patrick gave an apologetic half-smile and glanced between her and the volunteer. "I'm sorry. I was giving this big guy a bath, and he got away from me."

He looked at Tara. "Are you all right, miss? Did he scratch you?"

Katrina watched Tara's cheeks turn pink. "No, I'm all right."

Katrina quickly did introductions. "Patrick, this is my new volunteer, Tara. Tara, this is my friend Patrick. He's in charge of the dogs at Pet Friends, like I'm in charge of the cats."

Patrick nodded his head. "Nice to meet you, Tara. Hopefully, we will see a lot of you in the future."

Tara gave him a small shy smile and said quietly, "Likewise. Maybe we'll run into each other again." Patrick didn't seem to notice as the young woman's eyes followed him. He moved to approach Katrina, but looked down at the dog and backed up instead.

Patrick winced. "Katrina, is your cat all right? Are you okay? It looks like you got a few nasty scratches on your arms, and that one is bleeding a lot. Let me put this big oaf away and I'll swing by with the first-aid kit."

Katrina petted the cat, opened an empty cage, and gently laid the cat inside. "Thanks, Patrick. I'm fine, but I would appreciate you picking up the kit. And yes, the cat seems fine, just a little shaken up."

Patrick nodded his head. "Sounds good." He led the dog back to the canine area of the shelter.

Katrina turned to Tara, who was watching Patrick as he walked away. *It looks like Patrick has an admirer. How cute.* "How did the one-eyed cat get out? I thought she was in the cat socialization room?"

Tara averted her eyes. "I'm sorry, it's my fault she got loose. I was taking her back to her cage because the other cats kept picking on her. She was just trying to lie there and rest, and the others ones would come up on her blind side and pounce on her."

Laying a hand on Tara's shoulder, Katrina looked her in the eye. "You never have to apologize for taking care of one of these cats. Thank you for keeping an eye on her. You have been doing great for your first day."

Glancing back at the cat's cage, Katrina pursed her lips. "Although, I'm going to have to figure out what to do with this poor girl. She is such a sweetheart, but I too have noticed she's not thriving here. I'm just afraid that with one of her eyes missing, she won't find a forever home. I'm going to have to think about what to do with her."

After a moment's contemplation, Katrina turned back to Tara with a broad smile. "The cages you already cleaned out are positively sparkling. Do you mind continuing to clean out some more of the cat cages while their tenants are still socializing? I'd really appreciate it, and I'm sure they will too. I'm going to go to the back and get cleaned up so I don't get any infections or scare away potential adopters."

Tara's smile brightened. "Sure thing, you have me for another hour before I have to leave to head back to the college. I'll get right to work. I love working with these guys, even if it involves an awful lot of cleaning."

Katrina headed back to the break room and found Patrick digging through their first-aid kit. "Hey, I have some disinfectant and bandages. Wash the blood off, and then I'll help you with these."

Katrina walked over to the sink and washed her arms and face with soap and water. "You know, these are really superficial. I can handle this." She turned around and dabbed her face and arms dry with paper towels.

Shaking his head, Patrick approached with the bandages he'd prepared. "No. I want to take care of you. What are best friends for?" He placed a few bandages down the long scratches of her arm. He worked in silence for a few moments and then leaned down and gently kissed the bandage.

Katrina smiled up at him. "That's so much better. Thank you for taking care of me. It's great to know I can always count on you."

She was so lucky to have such an attentive best friend. He asked more quietly, "Hey, would you be free to get a few drinks with me after work tonight?"

Katrina smiled at him and replied casually, oblivious to his change in tone. "I would love to hang out, we have such a blast together, but can I take a raincheck? I have to get home tonight because I took on a new roommate, and it's going to take some time to get her settled."

Chapter Two

The Stranger on the Bus

They are going to love my new werewolf cat meme!

Katrina smiled to herself. Her slight figure hunching over her phone slowly sucked away her awareness. Her long red hair hung down around her face so only her slightly bulbous nose was visible behind the screen. She relaxed and let the noise of the public bus fade into the background.

Katrina logged into the local Loves Cats forum. She spent a few minutes scrolling through the latest posts. A tiny fuzzy kitten raised its paws like a holdup when someone pointed a finger at it, causing her to chuckle. Katrina sighed with concern as a fellow member talked about treating her cat for diabetes.

Scrolling through her own photos, Katrina finally found the one she was looking for. Her cat, Willa Randall, was a very ugly Lykoi werewolf cat. Her thin, wiry, gray-and-black fur had patches missing and one of her ears was stuck out at a weird angle. To Katrina, she looked like the most endearing cat she had ever seen.

Last year, poor Willa had sat unwanted at the shelter Katrina worked at. Finally, Katrina became fed up with people recoiling at the sight of her. Willa went home with Katrina, and the two of them got along like ice and cream. Willa had one of the most charming and quirkiest personalities Katrina ever met, and she adored her sweet Willa. By the way her photos and memes kept going viral, it seemed the internet did too.

Katrina went to hit the select button when the bus jerked to a stop. Her phone went flying and landed in the footwell of the seat in front of her.

Oh great, I hope I didn't crack my screen again!

Getting down on all fours, she was careful not to disturb the cat carrier next to her. One bright eye watched her intently as she stretched her arm, trying the reach the screen. The bus started up again, and the quick forward momentum slid the phone backwards under the seat behind her.

Katrina had little room to maneuver in the footwell of her bus seat, but she did her best to turn her body around and reach under the seat behind her. Her phone was nowhere to be seen.

Great, what do I do now? My stop is coming up, and I can't get off of this bus without my phone!

Katrina bumped her head as she climbed back into her bus seat. With her hair in disarray, Katrina looked up and noticed a man standing above her, watching her intently.

The man was thin, had black curly hair, and looked to be in his late twenties. He wore a very expensive business-casual outfit and pulled off a handsome geeky look, with his black thick-rimmed glasses and carefully trimmed stubble beard.

He held out Katrina's shimmery green phone as his surprisingly deep voice asked, "Is this what you were looking for? Unless you really wanted to know what type of shoes I wear?"

Katrina's face almost turned as red as her hair. She attempted to smooth the stray hairs back around her face as she gained her composure. She reached for her phone and mumbled, "Thank you. That last stop caught me by surprise."

Katrina glanced down at her phone and groaned inwardly. It was still on the Loves Cats forum page, but it looked like she'd accidentally posted a picture of the Easter cookies she baked the other day, instead of Willa.

The man curiously bent down and glanced into Katrina's pet carrier. She saw his eyes widen as he tripped over his own feet, trying to step back quickly as the large one-eyed cat glared at him.

It's a shame such a cute guy saw me crawling all over the floor of the bus. It wasn't exactly a good first impression. Oh well. It's not like I'm ever going to see him again.

The bus stopped again, and Katrina sighed in relief. *Saved by the bus stop.*

"This is my stop. Thank you for finding my phone." Katrina gently picked up the cat carrier from beside her feet and held it in front of her. She was careful not to bump it against any of the seats she passed by. Luckily, everyone seemed to get out of her way in a hurry when they saw the pet carrier coming toward them.

Katrina hopped off the last step of the bus and stepped off the walkway. She set down the pet carrier and picked up her phone in an attempt to do some damage control. Already the cookies she accidentally posted had dozens of comments.

People's remarks ranged from simple: "Where's Willa?", "Did Willa make the cookies?" to attacks of: "While those cookies look delicious, this is a cat forum. All non-cat-related discussions are to be posted on the non-cat thread."

One person even blamed her: "The cat-lovers group is usually a safe place where I can calm down from my busy day and relax with cute cat videos. Your cookies sent me on a binge that will set me back weeks. I don't know if I can trust the Loves Cats forum anymore."

Katrina groaned as she deleted the image.

I hope none of the moderators saw that.

If she wasn't careful, something like that could get her kicked off her favorite social media group, and that was the last thing she wanted. These people understood her. They all lived in the general area, loved their cats, and truly enjoyed sharing fun cat pictures with each other. They mourned the loss of each other's fur babies like no one else could understand. She didn't want to chance losing her virtual tribe.

Feeling too rattled to enjoy posting the meme she worked so hard on, Katrina saved it until later. Right now, it was time to get this one-eyed cat home. Katrina knelt in the grass and looked into the cat carrier.

The cat with one eye peered back at her. The second eye was a grotesque wound that was healed over, but it still made her stomach queasy when she looked at it.

Poor thing. She probably lost that eye in a fight. Now she's another misfit that no one wants to adopt.

Katrina talked into the cat carrier. "Hey, sweetie. How are you doing? I need to warn you. Our roommate looks scary on the outside, but I think you will get along with Willa splendidly. You don't need to worry. I will take care of you. You have a home now."

The calico cat's stomach moved of its own volition, trying to stretch in two different directions at once. *We better get you home.*

Chapter Three

Wolf

Katrina picked up the cat carrier and walked the few blocks to her apartment.

I'm going to have to come up with a more suitable name for you than the one-eyed cat.

She pulled out her keys and kept a careful watch at the base of the door as she slowly opened it.

Katrina quickly squeezed her body and the cat carrier through the doorway, preventing her scraggly looking cat from making a break for it.

Good cat. I do not feel like chasing you down the hallway today.

Once the cat realized there was no escape, she switched tactics to yowling loudly and rubbing her head against Katrina's ankles.

Katrina laughed. "Hello, Willa. I missed you, too. I know you must be hungry. You look like you are withering away since I fed you this morning. Well, today you are going to have to be patient for an extra few minutes. I will feed you as soon as I get our new roommate settled."

Katrina carried the cat carrier into her bedroom and sat it on the floor in the dark. Willa followed her, yowling loudly, so Katrina scooped up the werewolf cat and took her into the kitchen.

Maybe this will be easier if you are eating happily, instead of scaring that poor one-eyed cat.

Willa put her head into her empty food dish, as if willing food to appear magically. Katrina gently moved her out of the way in order to fill it with cat food. Willa knelt on her haunches, munching away, while Katrina hunted for another food and water bowl. She spun around at the sound of cat food spilling onto her kitchen floor. Katrina ran over to scoop up the bag. She found Willa inside, investigating the bag that was not normally left within her reach.

Stomach full, Willa went to lie down in her window box. The box had soft bedding covering the bottom of it and extended beyond the window so that Willa could lie in the sun and watch the birds to her heart's content.

After Katrina finished cleaning up her kitchen, she took the new food and water into her bedroom and closed the door to keep a curious Willa out. Katrina slowly opened the door to the pet carrier. The large calico cat stepped gingerly out of the cat carrier, her stomach nearly touching the ground. She sniffed at the food and water, not taking her good eye off of Katrina.

Katrina quietly crooned, "Welcome home, sweetie." Her voice startled the one-eye cat, and she ran under her bed. "Aww, you poor thing. Once you are comfortable, I will introduce you to your other roommate, Willa. I think you two will become fast friends, but we will not rush things. I know you have had a hard time lately."

Katrina set up a bed and litter box in her bedroom and left the one-eyed cat to get accustomed to her new surroundings in peace.

Looks cozy to me.

She took the blanket out of the pet carrier and set it outside of her bedroom to allow Willa to get used to the other cat's scent.

Katrina picked up her phone and logged into the Loves Cats Forum. A new message awaited her from user Catman007. His avatar was a cat dressed like Batman.

Hmmm... I wonder what this is about.

Catman007: Hello, I am a newbie on here and just wanted to let you know Willa's videos and memes caught my attention. I think they are hilarious. I can't wait for the next one.

Katrina replied with her username CuriousKat316. Her avatar was a picture of Willa looking at the world quizzically.

CuriousKat316: Always glad to meet another fan of Willa's! I am posting a new meme now, I'll tag you.

Katrina scrolled through her pictures. She found the photo of Willa jumping from the couch, her webbed Lykoi toes extended. She photoshopped bat wings onto Willa's back and posted it as "Bat Cat."

Immediately, her picture began getting likes, comments, and shares.

How satisfying.

Katrina smiled to herself. This was what she'd been expecting on her bus ride home. Willa curiously came to investigate the ping noises her phone was making.

She tried to move her onto her lap to cuddle, but within seconds, Willa was off investigating, sniffing around where she had set down the carrier and rolling on the blanket that was previously in that cage. Luckily, Willa couldn't get to the one-eyed cat through my bedroom door. She would let them get used to each other's scents, slowly at first. Katrina really wanted this to work out.

She was grinning to herself while scrolling through a story about a kitten surviving the Irish seas in a coffee can, when she received a text from Patrick.

Patrick: Hey, Katrina. You were in such a hurry to get out the door today that I didn't have time to say goodbye. Would you like to go kayaking with Groot and me this Saturday?

Katrina: I would love to, but I can't this week. I brought that one-eyed cat home with me and I need to spend 'Caturday' at home getting her settled in. I'm hoping to introduce her to Willa, but I need to keep a close eye on them to make sure they are getting along. Have fun with your dog.

Katrina ate her own dinner while watching a montage of kitten videos. Itty-bitty fluffballs tried to balance on things that they fell off of and tried to squeeze into the smallest of places. It made her feel good inside, like the day's troubles didn't matter anymore. Katrina's phone pinged.

Catman007: Hey, CuriousKat, love the new meme. Your cat is quite entertaining. I saw on your profile that you like puzzles. Did you see the cat riddle someone posted on the group chat? I tried to figure it out but got nowhere. Just thought you might enjoy it.

CuriousKat316: Thanks for the heads-up. I love a good mystery. I'll check it out!

Catman seems nice. I wonder what he looks like? Maybe he's a handsome cat lover who's just waiting to sweep me off my feet? But it's more likely he's a wart-covered, overzealous fan trying to get insider information about Willa.

Katrina went to check on the one-eyed cat whose one good eye slit open to watch her.

Her food is gone, and she is sprawled out on top of my bed. That's a good sign that she is getting comfortable.

The humongous belly of the cat jolted in different directions. She meowed piteously as she rolled onto her other side, as if trying to get comfortable. "You poor thing. You look so uncomfortable. Those kittens will be here any day now. I really hope I am home when you go into labor."

Chapter Four

Oliver and Company

Katrina checked her phone on her walk to work on Monday. She watched the cat-cam in her bedroom for a few minutes and sighed in relief. No kittens yet. This was going to be a long week if those babies didn't come soon!

She was almost to Pet Friends when she tripped over a box.

Oops, I wasn't paying attention to where I was walking again.

An angry yowl and warning growl came from the box.

Katrina slowly started to open the box to peer inside when sharp mud-covered claws attacked her hands through the hole in the top of the box.

Katrina backed up as the hissing continued. People passed her on the street, but no one was paying any attention to her. *Surely, there is someone around who cares about this animal trapped in the box?*

Gingerly, Katrina picked up the box and walked it the last block to work with her.

Apparently, whoever dumped their pet didn't bother to take them the extra few yards to the shelter. I have a few volunteers coming in today, but I'm not sure they can handle this cat.

Katrina juggled the box with one hand while attempting to open the door. Her best friend, a slim figure in a Pet Friends T-shirt, came over and held it for her.

"Patrick!" Katrina exclaimed. "You are just the person I was thinking of!"

Looking pleased, an enormous smile grew on Patrick's face.

Well, he is sure in a good mood.

"Feeling like you missed out on kayaking the other day? We can go again next weekend, as long as the weather holds out."

Katrina peered around the edge of the box. "Um… actually, I hoped you would help me give this cat a bath this morning. From the little I saw, the poor thing hasn't had a bath in a long time and is… personality challenged."

Patrick gave Katrina a frown. "What you are trying to tell me is that you have a dirty mean cat in that box and you are too afraid to ask your volunteers to help you. If you do, they will just quit."

Katrina's eyes grew large as she did her best to give an innocent look. "Does it help if I say please?"

Patrick grumbled, "I'll get my rubber gloves. That filthy creature probably has fleas, too."

Katrina smiled. "Yeah, probably." No matter how rough things got, Patrick was the one person she could always count on.

Katrina was readying a freshly cleaned cat cage when Patrick came over wearing a see-through plastic face shield and rubber gloves that went up to his elbows. Katrina couldn't help but let out a giggle.

Patrick raised his hands in mock surrender. "I learned my lesson after the last cat I helped you with. It scratched up my entire forearms while I helped you bathe it and splashed mucky water in my mouth. I'm determined that this cat will not get the best of me. Why you prefer cats over dogs is beyond my understanding."

Katrina put on her own pair of gloves and gently opened the box. An orange muck-covered tom as thin as bones attempted to jump out. Luckily, Katrina was ready. She grabbed the nape of his neck until Patrick got a good hold of him. The two of them supported and held the cat tightly while they transported him to a nearby utility tub filled with a few inches of soapy water.

Fleas covered the cat, indeed, and had caused his stomach to be covered in bright red, swollen sores. He growled deep in his throat and attempted to scratch and bite the two of them, even when it was having no effect through the thick rubber gloves.

Katrina saw pity in Patrick's eyes. "Poor guy. He looks horrible. No wonder he is so miserable. He has infections all over his stomach. He must be in such pain."

Katrina nodded as she focused on gently washing around the sores on her patient. "Yeah, I will call the veterinarian to take a look at Oliver. He is worse off than I expected."

Patrick raised an eyebrow at her from behind his face shield. "Oliver? I thought you just found this guy a few minutes ago."

Shrugging, Katrina continued her work. "He reminds me of that movie *Oliver and Company*, but only if that poor cat Oliver grew up on the streets and never found the little girl to dote on him."

Fur cleaned and brushed, Katrina admired the much calmer tomcat, Oliver. He was a handsome cat. She didn't think she would have any problem finding him a home after he healed up and became properly socialized. It might take a while, but there was still hope for him to have his happily ever after.

This was why she loved her job. Poor abandoned, mistreated, and lost cats without a hope came to her every day. It was her job to clean them up and care for them until she could find the perfect home for them. She truly believed there was a cat for every person; you just had to find the right pair.

After setting Oliver into his new temporary residence, Patrick asked, "So, how did the big cat introduction go at home this weekend?"

Katrina smiled and excitedly pulled her phone out of her pocket. "Well, I didn't leave them alone together today, because I didn't know how Willa would react if the new kittens came, but they were cuddling by the end of last night. Here is a picture of the two of them. Meet Captain Calico Jackie, my newest roommate."

Katrina pulled out a photo of her scraggly looking werewolf cat cuddled up next to the large calico cat, now sporting a black eye patch over her stitched-up eye socket. Surprisingly, the patch didn't seem to bother the cat at all. Katrina beamed at the picture of her fur-babies getting along so well.

Patrick looked at the picture. "Um… are you trying to curate an ugly cat collection? They will definitely scare off any intruders."

Katrina quickly took her phone away from Patrick. She gave him a playful glare. "You only look at the outside, but on the inside, these two are the sweetest cats in the world. You should be thankful to have half of their delightful personalities."

Patrick gave a playful huff. "Well, if you can't appreciate my humor, then I will find someone who does." Patrick lifted his head in the air as he stalked off to feed his canine charges.

Katrina stifled a giggle. While he may play tough, she had a feeling he would be back, asking to look at more photos before their shift was over. The two of them were inseparable. She really couldn't ask for a better friend.

After setting up Tara and her other volunteers to take turns socializing cats and cleaning their cages, Katrina took a lunch break. She washed her hands thoroughly after all the dirty work of the day and took a delicious-looking salad with chicken on top out of the fridge. Katrina took out her phone and logged onto the Loves Cats forum.

Pleased, Katrina saw another message from Catman. He sent her a joke about why you shouldn't play Monopoly with a cat... because they are *cheat-ahs*. Katrina couldn't help laughing a little at the corniness.

Katrina pulled up the puzzle that he'd sent her a few days ago. She finally had a few minutes to try to finish it. This was a hard one, but she loved a good riddle. She read it over again.

Five donuts for Henry

Four hot dogs for Carter

Eight street tacos for Miriam

Delivery's complete by Thursday at 6:00

How odd... it seems to give me an address. 548 Miriam Street. She looked up the address on the map app on her phone. *Interesting, there's a bench in the local dog park dedicated to a Henry Carter. That park is smack dab in the middle of the busy city. Hundreds of people walk through there every day. Some with pets and some just enjoying a walk. What is so important at that park that someone wrote a riddle leading there?*

Chapter Five

Bridget Jones's Diary

Katrina sang with a hint of a haunted twang in her voice as she crooned to the tune of *The Love Cats* by the Cure. She didn't have the most beautiful voice, but there were only a handful of people at the karaoke bar, so she didn't care. She was enjoying herself too much. When she finished, Patrick stood up and clapped loud enough for a whole crowd.

With a smile, Katrina plopped herself down beside him on a barstool. "Do you want to do a duet with me next?"

Patrick cocked his head and gave her a half-smile. "Maybe if I could have gone up first, but I don't think I can go up after you. I'll get booed off the stage."

Playfully swatting his shoulder, Katrina leaned over and picked up one of Patrick's curly fries. She said, "You don't need to be a scaredy-cat. I'm sure you can't be that bad." Then she plopped it into her mouth.

Patrick protested, "Hey, that was mine!" He rolled his eyes and pushed the basket of fries into the middle of the table. "So, how is your famous cat Willa doing? Are things still going well with that one-eyed one, too?"

Smiling, Katrina whipped out her phone. "Oh, you just have to see this adorable picture I posted in the Loves Cats forum of the two of them cuddled up in the window box." After spending a moment logging on and scrolling on her phone, she pushed it over for Patrick to see.

He picked up the phone and smiled when he saw the picture, and then he scrolled through the other recently posted threads. "They look cozy lying in the sun. You spoil them rotten. What I don't understand is how you could spend so much time on this social media page that's just about cats. Exactly how many times do you need to see napping cats?"

Katrina gave him a fake glare. "There are never enough napping cats in the world."

Patrick looked up from the phone. "Who exactly is Catman007? There are a lot of messages from him on here."

Cheeks turning slightly pink, Katrina took the phone back from him. "He's no one. Well, I'm sure he's someone. I just don't really know him. That's just someone I've been chatting with online a lot. I don't even know his real name."

Patrick's brow furrowed, and he crossed his arms. "You never know exactly who is on the other side of that internet conversation. Be careful and don't give him your name."

"Do you think there is a nefarious cat lover lurking in the Loves Cats forum? You don't need to be such a worrywart. He's just one of Willa's fans, and besides, I know how to keep safe." Katrina was a bit surprised at how concerned Patrick was over her innocent little conversations with Catman.

She was glad to have a best friend who was so concerned with her well-being, but she also decided not to mention the riddle Catman sent her that she was planning on investigating tomorrow night. She was dying to know if there really was something at the location she'd uncovered, and Patrick would just try to talk her out of going. *It's a public place. What harm could come of checking it out?*

Patrick shrugged, and they ate their fries in silence for a few moments as they listened to the current karaoke singer. Katrina knew she wasn't the best singer, but she didn't think she sounded that out of tune and off beat. It hurt her ears to listen.

Katrina tried to get the lighthearted atmosphere of their fun evening back. "Why are cats talented singers?"

Raising an eyebrow, Patrick said, "I don't know. Why?"

"Because they are *mewsical.*" Katrina chuckled at herself as Patrick smiled and shook his head.

Standing up, Patrick held out his hand to Katrina. "I think I'm ready to follow that act. Would you like to sing *I Got You Babe* by Sonny and Cher with me?"

Katrina smiled as she placed her hand in his and let him lead her to the stage. "Sure! I'm glad you're giving it a try. I've got you, babe. I'll sing extra loud if you get lost in the song."

The music started up, and Patrick sang in a smooth tenor that filled the room. In shock and a bit intimidated by his voice, Katrina's words barely came out in a whisper. Patrick took her hand and looked her in the eye as he nodded his head in encouragement. Focused on her partner, Katrina sang better than she ever had in her life as the deeper tone steadied her voice and her own rose above Patrick's in beautiful harmony.

When they finished, the small crowd gave them a standing ovation as they made their way back to their table.

Then the waiter came over. "You two sang great together. Your next drink is on the house."

Patrick and Katrina finished up their curly fries with their drinks. Patrick took a large gulp and then looked Katrina deeply in the eyes. "Katrina, I was wondering if you would—"

Katrina interrupted, "Don't worry, I know what's going on here. If you're about to ask my permission to ask my new volunteer out on a date, you don't need to worry because you already have my blessing. I saw the way Tara was eyeing you, and she seems really great. I never want to stand in the way of my best friend finding true love. Babe, I have you."

Looking down at the table, Patrick swished his drink around for a few moments. "Ah, thanks. Yeah. That's what I was going to ask."

Chapter Six

Dead Cat

Katrina hummed with excitement as she took a street taco from a vendor. Conveniently, there was a food truck right outside the park.

Is the food truck guy in on this riddle?

She gently tried to probe the short, balding man behind the counter.

Katrina slyly started up a conversation. "So, do you have any pet cats? You kind of look like a cat guy to me." Katrina gave him her most captivating smile.

The man looked at her in frustration. "Look, lady, I don't know what you are getting at. Let me cut to the chase because there are a lot of customers behind you. No, I do not use cats in my food, and no, I am not available. I'm married. Thank you for buying a taco. Please come again."

After that gruff dismissal, Katrina worked another angle to figure out the riddle. Katrina checked the time on her phone. It was almost six o'clock.

How exciting! This is almost like a scavenger hunt!

Katrina found a bench within easy view of the one dedicated to Henry Carter. She pulled up a binocular app on her phone and zoomed in on the bench. A thin well-dressed man with large sunglasses sat on the bench, nonchalantly staring at his phone. Katrina zoomed in and took a picture.

Sometimes you never know what is important in an investigation.

Six o'clock came and passed and nothing of interest happened. Katrina got mad at herself. She should have checked the bench. What if they attached something to the bench itself? Lots of people had walked by or paused by the water fountain next to the bench. Her hunt could be over already, and she missed it.

Maybe she'd missed a vital clue in the riddle? Was this a scavenger hunt she needed to find another clue to continue? Was there a geo-caching cache nearby? Maybe she needed to give a secret passcode to the taco vendor. *I should order a second street taco for my walk home. It was really delicious.*

It was ten minutes after six when Katrina stood up to leave. She needed to get back to her apartment. Her kitties would think they were starving to death. Katrina gave the Henry Carter bench a last glance before walking off.

A tall, muscular man wearing chain necklaces around his neck walked up to the bench with a pet carrier. Without saying a word, he set the pet carrier down and walked away. As soon as he was out of sight, the well-dressed man picked up the pet carrier without even looking inside.

Katrina followed the man at a distance. He nonchalantly carried the cage out of the park and disappeared into the subway. Confused and curiosity piqued, Katrina felt like this riddle had left her with more questions than answers.

What was in that pet carrier? Why would two totally different men exchange a pet that way? Isn't it odd that the two men didn't say a single word to each other? Why didn't I have my camera ready when something interesting happened?

Katrina logged onto the Loves Cats chat group on her bus ride home.

It's been such a weird evening, I need to recenter myself with cats.

An announcement showed a cat poetry contest coming up.

That's interesting, maybe I will have to try my hand at poetry.

She sent Catman a message.

CuriousKat316: Hey, Catman, I figured out that riddle.

Catman007: Really? What was it trying to say?

CuriousKat316: It was actually a location. A local dog park. I went and staked it out.

Catman007: You did what? You know, stakeouts should never be done alone. I wish you had told me because I would have joined you.

CuriousKat316: Ha-ha. You don't even know where I live. You probably live on the other side of the city from me.

Catman007: Just send me a message before you do something like that again. We don't want anything to happen to you. You never know what crazies you will find on the Internet. Did you see anything?

CuriousKat316: Well, I saw a guy pass off a pet carrier, but that's not odd at all in a dog park. I guess what caught me as weird was the fact that the guy didn't even bother to look inside the pet carrier. Usually, when I see someone get a new pet, they can't take their eyes off them.

Katrina's phone rang and she looked down at the caller ID. It was her landlord.

CuriousKat316: Landlords calling me. TTYL!

Katrina picked up her phone.

What in the world could he need? It was an older couple that owned the apartment she lived in. Did they lose her check? She would be home in about fifteen minutes. Couldn't it wait? He'd interrupted her in the middle of very important cat business.

Katrina answered, "Hello?"

An older gentleman on the line replied, "Katrina, I just got a call from your neighbor. They said they watched that stray cat of yours in your window that sticks out over the street. Your neighbor said your cat has been lying on her back with her feet sticking up for hours without moving. I'm sorry to be the one to tell you this, but we think she might be dead. I'll forward you the picture your neighbor took. She looks deceased to me."

He kindly prodded, "I'm sorry to be the one to tell you this, but you need to get home and make proper arrangements before she smells the place up. If you want, I can go in there and take care of things before you even get home."

Panic made Katrina's heart beat faster. Her breathing sped up, shorter and shallower. "I'll be home shortly. Thanks for letting me know." Katrina hung up and quickly brought the cat-cam up on her phone. She saw Captain Jackie sprawled out in her favorite position on her bed, locked in her bedroom for the day. Unfortunately, Katrina had no way of checking on Willa.

Her poor Willa, tears ran down Katrina's face. She wanted to hold and cuddle her fur-baby. Nothing else could make this all right.

Can't this bus drive any faster?

Chapter Seven

The Cat from Outer Space

"These cats are great and all, but none of them are a dog," the young boy with shaggy brown hair sadly told Katrina. "I'm glad Mom said I could get a pet, but what I really want is a dog, and Mom says I can't have one because I'm allergic."

His mother's wide eyes looked apologetic, but she shrugged. "I thought it would be good for Timmy to have a pet to take care of and learn responsibility. When I told him we would come and look at cats today, I didn't get the excited response I was hoping for. We should probably just leave. I don't want to waste your time."

Katrina shook her head and waved a hand to dismiss the thought. "Don't worry about wasting our time. We are here to introduce people to pets and find the perfect matches. Why don't we just look together and see what we find? If we don't find a good match, you can always leave after taking a peek." The mother nodded, so Katrina knelt down in front of the boy. "Timmy, why do you want a dog? What is it you like about them?" Katrina asked.

The boy furrowed his brow as he thought for a moment. "I want a dog who will be excited to see me when I get home from school, and I want to play with him and stuff. I don't want a cat because they just lie around and are boring."

Katrina smiled and led the boy to a cage with a sleek tan cat. The mother followed silently. "Timmy, I would like to introduce you to Zunar-J5/9-Doric-48." Katrina smiled at his confusion. "Don't worry, you can call him Jake for short. This is not just an ordinary cat, but a cat from outer space. He can't return home and needs someone to take care of him."

Katrina pulled out a sparkling collar she'd found specifically for Jake. She opened the cage and put the collar around his neck and then held him out toward Tim. "Go ahead and pet him. Jake is an extremely friendly, extroverted cat who would be very excited when his owner got home every day."

Katrina pulled out a stick with a feather dangling from it from a nearby shelf and handed it to the boy. Immediately, the cat in Katrina's arms squirmed around, trying to bat at the toy. "Would you like to spend some time playing with Jake? We have special playrooms we can put you guys in where you can spend some time getting to know each other."

Timmy watched the cat for a few moments and then looked at Katrina with his brows raised. "That outer-space stuff is just pretend, right?"

Katrina smiled as Jake butted his head against her hand, demanding to be petted, before reaching his paw back out to bat at the feather dangling from the stick Timmy held. "Jake is a one-of-a-kind cat, but yes, the outer-space part is pretend. Do you want to meet him?"

Timmy nodded his head and gave a slow smile as the cat meowed at him and leaned into his petting. "Yeah, I guess. I mean, he looks like a friendly cat, and he needs a home." Timmy held the feather up before Jake, who lightly batted at it with his paws. "Yeah, I want to play with him."

Katrina led Tim and his mother to one of the private playrooms. *I think they just met their future cat. They look good for each other. I love it when I get to see a happy future for one of my charges.*

Patrick came over to stand beside Katrina and watch Timmy playing with the cat. "Looks like you found a home for another one. It's a shame he has allergies, or I would have totally beaten you to that adoption."

Katrina smiled. "I'm just glad to find a good match. Hey, I forgot to grab a lunch today. Would you like to go to the hotdog stand down the street with me for lunch?"

An enormous smile grew on Patrick's face. "Sure, I would love that. Give me fifteen minutes?"

Katrina nodded. "Yeah, sure. I'm so glad you can join me. There are a few things I wanted to talk to you about. Just wait until you hear my story about how Willa slept in her window box like a dead bug and the landlord called me. I also am considering meeting that guy, Catman, in person. I really like him and want to bounce some thoughts off you."

Patrick turned and walked away. He mumbled an unenthusiastic, "Yeah, can't wait to hear *all* about him. I'll be back in fifteen."

That evening after work, an exhausted Katrina dragged herself to the bus station.

I hope Catman is online tonight. He always makes me smile when we chat on my commute home. He has been throwing around a lot of hints about meeting in person. As long as we meet in a public place, it should be fine. Right?

Katrina boarded the bus. It was pretty close to capacity, but she found a seat. A few rows behind her, she noticed the man who'd found her phone under the bus seats a few weeks ago. He was busy staring into his phone and didn't seem to notice her.

Katrina sat down and opened her phone. She smiled when she saw the background. It was a picture of the movie *The Wolfman. I don't understand anyone who doesn't enjoy old movies.* She logged onto the Loves Cats forum. A message popped up from Catman. He was online right now.

Catman007: Guess what! I found another puzzle that reminded me of the one that took you to the dog park.

CuriousKat316: Really? I'm dying to know what is going on with those puzzles. Send it to me and I will see if I can figure it out.

Catman007: I will send it to you, under one condition.

Curious Kat316: A condition? I don't like the sound of that.

Catman007: It's nothing bad, you just have to take me with you. Once you solve the puzzle, don't go running off on your own. Tell me, and we will go together.

Katrina's gaze drifted from her phone. Right now, Catman was a theoretical person she could daydream about.

I don't even know his real name! Do I really want to meet him in person? On one hand, if he really was covered in warts, he wouldn't want to meet in person. Do I want to risk losing my virtual friend?

Catman was like a riddle that she didn't know if she wanted to solve. There was a reason she chose CuriousKat for her username. Katrina loved a good puzzle... but where would this one lead her?

Chapter Eight

Pet Shop

The sun shone down on Katrina. She lifted her head up to the sun, soaking up the rays. *What a nice day it is today. I have to take advantage of such a beautiful day. It's my day off, and the past few days have been so rainy and overcast.*

Katrina called behind her, "Willa, how are you doing back there? Are you enjoying the sunshine too?"

Willa replied with a soft meow in agreement. She perched on her hind legs in a cat backpack, looking at the world through the plastic bubble. Katrina was glad she went in the backpack at all after the debacle they'd had the first time they took it out.

Maybe she should invite Patrick to go out for a walk with her and Willa? He was always inviting her to go kayaking or hiking with him and his dog, and he was such a good listener. She'd never met a guy who did such a good job hearing what she had to say without trying to fix everything. Although, he didn't seem to be the biggest fan of Catman007.

I wonder why.

Katrina picked a well-populated street to turn down at random. She didn't particularly care where she ended up. The walk itself was the destination. After passing a building called Grover's Pet Store, she stopped dead in her tracks. She recalled the latest puzzle from the Loves Cats forum.

Meet at one o'clock, not at two

Go to buy a leash or three

Grover has the best

New stock comes on Thursday

That must be the place the riddle was talking about! Should she go inside? She knew she told Catman that she would go to the next meeting with him. This would just be scoping out the area, right? Having convinced herself that it was morally right to enter the pet store, she opened the door.

A bell jingled overhead, and Katrina heard a few birds squawking from the back of the store. Otherwise, the store was empty except for an overweight gentleman who stood behind the counter. The shelves were jam-packed with pet supplies. It was all well organized, but there were so many stands and baskets of items on sale that it felt very compact.

"Hello, my dear! Welcome to Grover's Pet Store. I'm James Grover. How can I help you today?" James cheerily greeted her.

Katrina ducked her head. She was expecting to slip in, look around, and head back out, with no one really noticing her. "Hello, my cat and I were out for a walk and passed your store. We were just stopping in for a look around. I'm sure I will have no problem finding the cat snacks."

James came out from behind the counter. "You know, your hair reminds me of a picture of my aunt Zelda when she was younger.

What a striking, vibrant red." He peered into the backpack through the plastic bubble, and Willa stared back at him. "Who is this? She's not your ordinary type of cat now, is she? What's her name? Do you mind if I give her a cat treat?"

This visit was getting more personal than she'd planned. Should she tell him the truth or make up a name? It didn't really matter. It wasn't like she was going to bring Willa back to the stakeout. Besides, it was nice when someone became excited to meet Willa.

Katrina put on an enormous smile. "This is Willa, she's a Lykoi cat. Yes, she can have a treat."

James grabbed a bag of cat treats from a shelf. "Willa! She's not *the* Willa from the Loves Cats forum, is she?"

Katrina's eyes grew wide, and she smiled more shyly from embarrassment. "Yes, this little bundle of personality is the one and only Willa."

James handed the bag of cat treats into Katrina's hands and walked behind her again to study Willa closer.

It is really odd having conversations with people standing behind me.

"Well, I'll be. That cat always makes me smile. You can have the entire bag on the house. Is there anything else I can help you with?"

Katrina looked around, trying to get her bearing. "I was hoping to take a peek at your leashes. I have a friend who recently got a new dog, and I told him I would grab one at the store for him. Could you point me in the right direction? Also, when do you receive new shipments of supplies?"

James looked at Katrina curiously, but didn't ask questions. "My next truck comes on Tuesday, but don't worry. I have a wide selection of leashes in stock. Follow me."

James led her to the leash aisle. It looked like a completely normal leash aisle to Katrina. James turned to walk away, but she quickly asked him, "Do you get anything in on Thursday?"

James shook his head. "No, I specifically don't want any of my orders coming in on Thursdays. We host cat adoptions at 2:00 in the afternoon that day, and I'm always so busy with all the people coming and going. I couldn't handle another thing going on."

"Thanks. You have been very helpful," Katrina told him. She went back to pretending to look at leashes.

Should I buy a leash for my cover story?

Looking up at the clock, she noticed that the time was an hour off. It probably never got changed with the last daylight savings change.

Interesting. The riddle said, meet at 1:00, not at 2:00. I wonder if I have to come an hour early, like the pet store's clock, or else I will miss whatever is going to happen.

She got out her phone to check the cat-cam in her bedroom. She checked it so often it was feeling like second nature. *Let's see how Captain Jackie is doing.* As she logged on, Katrina's mind wandered.

Maybe I should message Catman and set up a time to meet him before we stake out the pet store together. Just to feel him out and get to know him. I mean, I can't continue to call him Catman forever. It's feeling ridiculous now that we have more of a friendship.

She looked at her phone for a few minutes, not registering what she saw. There was Jackie, breathing heavily, licking a tiny wet kitten.

It's time! I need to get home now!

Willa yowled in protest as Katrina whipped around and quickly speed-walked to the front of the store. She rushed out the door in a flurry, leaving behind a very puzzled store owner.

Chapter Nine

Kitty Mamas

Katrina rushed up the stairs and into her apartment. She quickly released Willa from her backpack and impatiently poured her food. Deep breaths. She needed to calm down before she got into her bedroom. She didn't want to scare the new momma or her babies.

Katrina finally felt ready to sneak stealthily into her bedroom. She left Willa out in the main part of her apartment. *No need to add stress to Captain Calico Jackie's labor by bringing in that furry attention hog. Besides, I'm not sure how Willa will react to even more cats on her home turf.*

Captain Jackie lay sprawled out on the special bed Katrina had made for her. She'd lined it with puppy pads to absorb any liquids and covered it with soft disposable rags and towels. She was hoping to make post-birth cleanup as easy as possible.

The cat's paws kneaded the blankets in front of her as three tiny blind kittens nursed eagerly. So far, the largest kitten was gray and white. There was also a coal-black kitten and a calico kitten that still looked damp. Captain Jackie watched Katrina entering the room, but she didn't seem to mind.

Softly Katrina crooned, "Hello, Jackie. You are doing such a good job being a momma. Look at those precious babies. What do you think of the names Drake for the gray and white, Cal for the calico, and Sam for the black one? They are still so little that we can always adjust their names once we can tell their genders."

Captain Jackie's single good eye landed on Katrina and stared at her as her abdomen moved in rhythm with another set of contractions. Her breathing grew slightly heavier. Her eye patch currently hung on a shelf behind her. Katrina had decided a while ago to keep her comfortable when it was just them at home. The eye patch would be for looking fancy when they had company over.

Katrina watched in fascination as another sleek, wet black kitten emerged. Jackie moved around to lick her new baby clean. The dislodged kittens began softly mewling as they tried to get back to their dinner. Jackie picked one kitten up gently in her mouth by the back of the neck and held it up toward Katrina.

"Oh, Jackie, they are absolutely precious. Thank you for showing them to me. You are such a sweet cat, and I can tell that you are going to be such a good mama to those four little babies."

Katrina reached down to pet Jackie, who leaned into the touch. Cautiously, Katrina reached down to pet one of the dry kittens. Jackie continued to purr as she arranged herself and laid back on the bed. The kittens struggled to get closer to their mother and nursed one by one.

Katrina took a few photos and a short video of the new little family. She labeled them "Kitten Day" and posted them on the Loves Cats forum. One of the first people to comment said, "You have to be kitten me."

She rolled her eyes. *People think they are so clever.*

"Well, Jackie, you have been working hard in here. I will let you guys rest. Why don't I get fresh bedding ready for you and your kitties? I'll be back in a bit to check on you again," Katrina said as she slowly and carefully moved out of the room.

Outside her bedroom door, Willa sat waiting expectantly. *Apparently, she knows something is going on in there.*

"Willa, guess what? You are an aunt! We are going to give the babies a few days to get used to living outside the womb while I bring some bedding out here for you to smell and help you get used to everyone. Then we will do some careful introductions to see how you guys get along. Sound like a plan?"

Katrina's phone beeped.

Catman007: Congratulations on the new kittens. Are we still on for Thursday?

CuriousKat316: That's still a few days off. My mama cat seems to be doing a great job. All four kittens look healthy, so I plan to follow this riddle rabbit regardless of what hole he takes me down.

CuriousKat316: Although, I was thinking about it. I would like to meet you before the stakeout. Would you be free on Wednesday night?

Catman007: Sounds like a great idea. Yes, I'm free. Would you like to meet at the little bistro at the intersection of 3rd and Park?

CuriousKat316: Sure. I'm not familiar with it, but I'm sure I can find it. We should do something so we recognize each other. How about we both wear green shirts?

Catman007: Sure, I'll wear my best. I'll have a flower to help identify me, too.

CuriousKat316: Great! Since that is settled, I really should get back to this new mama. Bye!

Katrina put down her phone and started gathering together fresh cat bedding, food, and water. She hummed with excitement. *Time to visit the new kitties!* She slowly opened the door, keeping Willa out again.

To her surprise, there were two more kittens snuggled up next to Jackie, nursing. Both were identical, with orange-and-white stripes. One was lying on top of a sibling in order to reach a nipple that was higher up.

Katrina muttered to the mama cat, "Looks like you have more surprises for me, Captain Jackie. That's a lot of kittens you were carrying around. You poor thing, no wonder you were so uncomfortable. Here is some fresh food and water for you, but maybe we will wait a little before changing out your bedding? Just in case. These two new babies look like a Bonney and a Mary to me. Although, I'm not sure how I will tell them apart. Maybe Bonney looks more like a boy? I'm pretty sure most orange cats are boys... oh well, I can always change the names later."

Jackie meowed loudly and stood up. The kittens nosed around, mewling, trying to find their way back to their mother. She took a moment to rub up against Katrina in appreciation. She ate and drank heartily for a few moments and then returned to her kittens.

Jackie's contractions started again, and Katrina gave her a bit of space. *Now that is going to be one busy cat with all of those kittens.* Katrina made her own dinner, while constantly checking the cat-cam to see if there were any more developments.

A white kitten was born, followed shortly by an itty- bitty black-and-white kitten. *The white one will be Thomas and the runt will be Bart.* Slowly, the white kitten made its way over to join his siblings and nurse. The black-and-white kitten just laid there, too exhausted from birth to move.

Chapter Ten

Chicken Soup

Katrina rushed around work after hours, searching for the kitten equipment she needed. This wasn't the first time she'd needed it. Sometimes a litter of kittens were brought in without the mother before they were ready to wean. Sometimes she would get a sick kitten. Regardless, she had to hurry before she was too late for Bart.

Katrina found a large box containing a kitten incubator. It was large and would be awkward carrying onto the bus, at roughly forty pounds, but she needed it and had to make it work. She had thought about having Patrick take it to her apartment ahead of time, just in case, but was too worried she would then need it at the shelter. Luckily, at least it wasn't occupied right now, and she could take it to where she needed it most.

She set it by the door as she frantically searched around for the small tube she used for feeding baby kittens directly to their bellies and KMR or Kitten Milk Replacement. She knew she'd put it back the last time she needed it, and that was weeks ago. What if one of her volunteers had used the rest of it without discussing it with her?

Her mind ran to the worst-case scenario of not finding the equipment. She truly didn't think Bart would make it, and she didn't know where else she could get the KMR at this time of night. It wasn't like she could just run to the grocery store. Cow milk would give the poor kitten an upset stomach. She really hoped she didn't have to express milk from a cat. She was not even sure Captain Jackie would let her, and she wouldn't blame her.

There, pushed to the back of the shelf, was a single bottle of KMR left. She yelled out a delighted, "Found it!" before she grabbed it and the nearby tube and shoved them both into her backpack. She could always get more KMR tomorrow when the pet stores were open. This was plenty for now.

In a hurry, she turned off the lights of the shelter and locked the door behind her. Before she left, she had put Bart up against his mother, but he still didn't seem to suckle strongly like the other kittens. *I hope I'm not too late!*

On the bus ride home, she texted the owner of the shelter to let her know she'd borrowed the kitten supplies and would most likely need to take a sick day the next day. Then she sent Patrick a quick message saying that she wouldn't be in tomorrow and asking him to direct her volunteers for the day.

When she finally got to her apartment, she lugged the incubator up the stairs and groaned internally when she saw Mrs. Danglehauser. *Oh no! I don't have an hour to reminisce about something mundane, like the clouds or something.*

Mrs. Danglehouser opened her mouth, but before her neighbor could say a word, Katrina interrupted as she continued to speed along.

"I'm sorry, Mrs. Danglehauser, I can't talk right now. There is a kitten emergency going on. We will catch up soon. Have a good night."

Flustered, Mrs. Danglehouser simply responded with a, "Good night, dear. I will pray for your emergency."

Katrina opened her door, dumped her supplies on the table, and quickly left to check on Bart. He was still alive but had gotten pushed away from his mother again. Katrina helped him back to his mother. She at least needed to keep him warm until she could heat the incubator up. Then she left to prepare supplies.

She turned on the kitten incubator, prepared the KMR, and went to check on the kittens. They were all doing fine, except Bart. He still wasn't nursing on his own. She scooped him up and put him against her skin to keep him warm as she carried him to the incubator. He mewled pitifully, and it broke her heart. *At least he has the energy to complain. That's a good sign. I will have to bring some siblings over to join him after they have finished eating.*

After she warmed Bart up, Katrina took out the KMR and tube to feed him. Before long, his little belly was well rounded. *Much better.* She set the little guy back into the incubator and grabbed a few napping kittens from Jackie. They snuggled together in the incubator and fell fast asleep.

Over the next evening and the next day, she set a timer to get up every two hours to check on the kittens and hand feed Bart. Willa seemed to enjoy the night-time attention and brought Katrina toys to play with as she fed the kitten. Exhausted and blurry-eyed, she did her best to play but ended up slumped on the couch.

She tried to nap between feedings, but despite being tired, by the time she would fall asleep, it was time to wake up again. Eventually, she gave up and watched a show. What she watched, she really didn't know. She was too tired to follow the plot fully.

Night blurred into day. He seemed to improve and was getting around better on his own, but he still wasn't nursing. When the kitten was with his mother, she would clean him and he would nestle up to her. He just couldn't seem to latch on well enough to eat.

After feeding and putting Bart back into the incubator, Katrina got up to make herself some food. *I'm too tired for proper food. What if I just eat some ice cream for dinner? I've worked hard enough to enjoy a splurge, right?* She grabbed a pint of ice cream, took the lid off, and stuck a spoon directly into it.

She heard a knock on her apartment door. *It's probably Mrs. Danglehouser checking in on my kitten emergency.* Carrying her ice cream with her to the door, Katrina looked at herself in the entryway mirror before opening it.

Her hair was greasy and messy. Her clothing was covered in cat hair, kitten formula, and who knew what else. *I really should change before I talk to Mrs. D.* Too tired to care, Katrina opened the door.

There stood Patrick with a plastic container full of soup of some sort. Katrina saw shock register on his face as he saw the dark circles under her eyes and the state of disarray her hair and clothing were in.

He held up the container, eyed her pint of ice cream, and cautiously said, "Amy said that you took a sick day today. I was happy to help organize your volunteers, but I also thought I would stop by and drop off some chicken noodle soup. I'm glad I did. You look like you could really use it."

Chapter Eleven

The Rescuers

Katrina woke from the most wonderful nap she'd ever taken. She felt so good that she wanted to just stay and snuggle into her bed. She heard a small mewling and everything came flooding back to her. *Bart!*

She looked at the clock. It was two in the morning. *How could I sleep that long?* Katrina knelt down and petted Captain Jackie. She purred happily, kneading at her clean bedding. Six little fuzzy kittens stepped over each other and kneaded at their mother's stomach as they nursed.

Katrina stroked her soft fur. "These six look healthy. Good job, Mama. Keep up the hard work." *I'm going to have to get her spayed after these little ones wean. She is doing a fantastic job as a mother, but I already have a full-time job finding homes for cats.*

Katrina padded quietly out into the living room. Lying on the couch, oblivious to the world, was Patrick. He snored loudly while Willa laid curled up on his legs. She opened one eye to peer at her but was too comfortable to move. *Aww... they look so cute together. I can't believe he stayed this long. He really is a good friend.*

Earlier in the afternoon, when he stopped by to drop off chicken noodle soup, Katrina told him all about the neonatal kitten and how she had to feed him every two hours because he wasn't latching correctly and eating on his own.

Sweet Patrick volunteered to take over the next feeding so that she could take a shower and get a bit of rest. Katrina's exhausted body agreed, and she used the next feeding to show him exactly what to do. That was seven hours ago. She gently tucked him in with an extra blanket.

Bart was sleeping in the incubator, intermittently moving around one of his legs or head during his dreams. Katrina scooped him up and took him back to his mother. She hoped if he kept trying to nurse, eventually he would be strong enough to do it on his own.

Katrina took the kitten back to her bedroom and set him down beside Jackie, who licked her baby in greeting. Bart mewled as he climbed on top of Cal and used him as a stool to reach one of the higher nipples. Katrina could have danced in excitement and pride as he latched on and suckled greedily. *Hopefully, we are over the hump!*

Katrina heard an alarm as Patrick's phone went off. She heard a panicked exclamation from her bedroom. "Oh, no! I lost the kitten. Katrina's going to kill me!"

Katrina hurried out to the living room to reassure him. "Don't worry! Bart is successfully nursing in my bedroom. All of our hard work paid off! Thank you so much for giving me a break and caring for Bart. You should have woken me. I never expected you to stay so long."

Blurry-eyed, Patrick looked at her. "How are you feeling? You look much better."

Katrina smiled. "I feel so much better, although you look like a mess now. Would you like me to heat you up some chicken noodle soup? I have some that is really delicious in my fridge."

Patrick shook his head. "No, I'm good. I should probably get going. I need to get some sleep before work tomorrow."

Katrina pointed to the couch. "If you wanted to stay, the couch is free, and I make a mean omelet in the morning."

Patrick sadly shook his head. "No. My dog, Groot, will be waiting up for me. I need to let him out tonight and feed him tomorrow morning." Sarcastically he added, "We don't all have the luxury of calling in sick whenever we have a pet to care for."

"Fine, fine. Thank you so much, Patrick. It really means a lot to me that you stayed. You are truly the best friend a girl could wish for." *Patrick is so kind. I don't think I would have made it another eight hours of interrupted sleep. How in the world can I make it up to him?*

There is one thing that he keeps asking me to do that I push off. Time to suck it up and buy a life jacket.

"You know, I'm free Saturday morning if you still wanted to go kayaking?"

A huge grin spread across Patrick's face. "That would be fun. Groot would love to meet you. Do you think you will be at work this week to discuss details?"

Katrina nodded her head. "I need to keep a close eye on Bart the rest of tonight and tomorrow morning. As long as he continues to eat and cuddle up with his siblings, then I'm thinking I will be back tomorrow later in the afternoon. It's nice when volunteers help, and Tara is very nice, but it always seems like the work just keeps piling up when I take a day off. See you in a handful of hours."

As Patrick was leaving, he smiled at her as he flippantly remarked, "You know, these cats of yours were splendid company tonight. I can see why you are so attached to them. There is only one thing that would make them even better... if they were dogs."

Katrina groaned as he exited the door. She checked to make sure that all the kittens were doing well, but felt too keyed up to go back to bed. She made herself some chamomile tea and started working on a poem for the Loves Cats poetry contest. After wrinkling up and discarding her third attempt at poetry, she decided she wasn't in the right mindset right now.

She went to her bedroom and started pulling out every piece of bulky clothing and any accessories that she wouldn't normally wear. She threw them on her bed, and the piles of hats, scarves, sunglasses, and jackets grew. *I can't believe there is this much in my closet that I don't wear. I should make a clothing donation when I'm done finding the perfect disguise.*

Chapter Twelve

Sherlock Holmes

Katrina rounded the bend of Park Lane, glancing behind her. It was a pretty shady area. *What does that say about Catman that he wanted to meet here? Should I call the whole thing off?*

She came up to the intersection of 3rd Street. Her curiosity got the best of her. *It can't hurt to just meet him, right?* There wasn't anywhere to eat exactly on the corner of the two streets, but there was a small seedy-looking diner not far across the street. *That's the closest restaurant, I guess that's it.*

A bell jingled as she walked into the diner. She looked around anxiously for someone wearing a green shirt and holding a flower. No one looked up and greeted her, so she studied the customers more closely.

Finally, her eyes landed on an older man with an enormous beer belly. He was wearing a stained green T-shirt with a bit of cat hair on it and there was a wilted daisy decorating the table in front of him. He was munching down on a large fish sandwich, oblivious to the rest of the world.

He was not exactly what she was hoping for, but at least warts didn't cover his whole body or something equally as gross. *I should give him a chance. He's not the striking young man of my daydreams, but anyone can love cats. I'm sure we will have a lot to talk about.*

Katrina took a deep breath and bravely walked over to the stranger. She sat in the seat across from him. He looked up as Katrina started the conversation with a nervous string of consciousness. "Hello, my name is Katrina. It's very nice to meet you. Your fish sandwich looks good. I think I will get one as well. Although, when we get home, our cats might get jealous. Right?"

When the man just stared at her and didn't answer, she tried another approach. "Are you ready to unveil the mystery? What's your real name?"

The man chewed for a few minutes, staring at her before he answered.

Looks like he's a man of few words. Maybe he just types faster than he talks.

"Nice to meet you, too. My name is Pete. I have a cat. How did you know? Are you some kind of Sherlock Holmes or something?"

Katrina looked embarrassed. "Well, we both know that I love a good puzzle, but I have a long way to go until I can match that character. Do you enjoy Arthur Doyle's works? To answer your question, how could you love cats so much and not have one of your own?"

Pete stared at Katrina with a perplexed look on his face. He was saved from having to answer when a waitress in a stained apron came over with a notepad. She chewed her gum loudly as she asked, "What can I get ya?"

Katrina looked over at Pete's plate and ordered. "I think I will have a fish sandwich, too. With a water, please."

"Coming up," the waitress replied as she walked away.

Katrina turned back to Pete. "Are you going to enter the poetry contest? I only have a few more days to finish my poem, and I can't think of anything good."

Pete took a drink of his soda and made a loud slurping sound when the glass was almost empty. "Do I look like I write poetry? I would rather use thumb screws on myself than write poetry."

"Oh." Crestfallen, Katrina didn't know how to respond to that. This conversation wasn't going at all like she thought.

He sounds like a completely different person online than in real life. I guess that just goes to show that you don't really know anyone online.

The waitress brought back a fish sandwich for Katrina. She politely replied, "Thank you." The bread was hard, the lettuce drooped, and the fish was lukewarm.

That was really fast. I wonder if she just microwaved it back there.

Pete stared at her, looking uncomfortable, and kept chewing, not making any effort to engage her in conversation.

He was the one who suggested meeting in the first place. Now he's acting like I've just interrupted his meal.

Katrina forced herself to take a bite of the sandwich. If her mouth was full, she wouldn't have to come up with another topic to discuss. *This conversation is getting painful. I should have canceled.*

Katrina's phone beeped. *Saved by the bell!* With a sigh of relief, she excused herself. "I'm so sorry, Pete. It was really nice to meet you, but a cat emergency came up at work and I need to go. Hopefully, I will see you around in the forum soon."

Katrina dug around in her wallet and left enough cash on the table to cover her mostly uneaten sandwich and the tip. Then she slipped out the door. She walked down the street out of sight before getting her phone out to see who messaged her.

Catman007: Did you forget about dinner or are just running late?

CuriousKat316: Is this some kind of joke, Pete? I just ate with you, and you barely said a few words to me.

Catman007: I'm not Pete... where exactly are you?

CuriousKat316: Are you trying to tell me you gave me another fake name for you? I'm currently walking away from the little diner you invited me to as fast as I can. I'm not coming back to Park Lane and 3rd Street again.

Catman007: That's not a very nice area. You should leave before you get mugged. I have been waiting for you at the fancy bistro at the intersection of Park Boulevard and 3rd Avenue.

Katrina stopped stock still as heat rose to her cheeks. Poor Pete, she had just rudely interrupted his meal. What must he think of her? What was Catman thinking when she never showed up to meet him?

Catman007: At least I know I wasn't stood up. Do you want to try meeting again? This time you name the time and place and I will come to you. Just make sure it isn't somewhere we will get robbed.

CuriousKat316: Let's meet tomorrow at lunch time outside of Alex's Costume Store. It's a quick walk to the pet store and that will give us a bit of time to plan before we go to unravel this mystery. Something fishy is going on, and I am determined to understand it.

Chapter Thirteen

Pink Panther

Thursday at work was a slower day. There were a few volunteers helping her clean cages and feed her charges, but nothing too out of the ordinary. Tara was picking everything up so well that Katrina let her go when she started directing some of the other volunteers on what they should do next. She would make a great girlfriend for Patrick if he ever got the courage to ask her out.

Captain Jackie, Bart, and the other kittens were doing great, so she felt comfortable leaving them for the whole day. It tickled her pink to notate Bart's weight increases. Things could have gone either way for the little fellow, so it was good to see him gaining consistently. It also made her feel better to know she could still check on them through the camera she'd installed in her bedroom to check in on them anytime she needed.

One younger man came in looking for a cat for his daughter. He didn't seem to care too much about the personality or look of the cat, as long as it was fluffy. He came in, filled out adoption papers, and walked out with an orange long-haired cat named Jonesy roughly fifteen minutes later. One of the fastest and easiest adoptions she'd ever completed.

Before long, it was lunchtime. She requested the rest of her day off so she could take her time getting to know Catman and solve the riddle. *I will sort this out! It's probably something silly, and once I figure it out, I will laugh about how much time and effort I put into these riddles.*

Katrina made her way to Alex's Costume Store. She was carrying a large bag full of an assortment of sweaters and hats.

Katrina waited across the street, trying to keep her feet from fidgeting. She'd learned her lesson from her last meeting, and now she was nervous. *Catman wasn't Pete, but what if he's worse?* She wasn't looking forward to this meeting anymore.

She watched many customers walk up to the hot dog stand outside of the costume store and take their purchases on the way to their next destination. One particularly well-dressed gentleman stopped at the hot dog stand and looked around. He looked out of place and dressed for a much nicer establishment in his dark green dress shirt. He held in his hand a single red rose. *Catman.*

The thin man had curly black hair. His carefully trimmed stubble beard and thick black-rimmed glasses gave him a handsome techie kind of look. It was the man she'd met on the bus weeks ago.

Catman has been the man on the bus this whole time!

He locked eyes with her across the street, clearly recognizing her. His eyes didn't leave her as he jogged across the street. As he neared, his smile grew. He handed her the rose and gave her a self-satisfied smile. "Hello, I guess the cat is out of the bag. You know who I am now. My name is Jared."

Katrina narrowed her eyes at him. "Jared, nice to meet you. How did you find me after meeting on the bus? I can't believe it was just chance that we ran into each other on the Loves Cats forum right after I met you on the bus."

Jared looked down at his feet and rubbed the back of his neck. "In all honesty, it wasn't an accident. That day on the bus, I saw the most beautiful and intriguing woman and I just had to meet you. When I picked up your phone, I saw a forum on it called Loves Cats. I saw you posting under the name CuriousKat and didn't know how else to get in touch with you again, so I joined to get to know you."

Jared looked up at her through his eyelashes. "You aren't mad at me, are you?"

Katrina pursed her lips. She wasn't pleased that he didn't announce himself, but she did really enjoy talking to him online. She would miss him if she just cut him off now, and he looked sincere. "All right, I will forgive you, but this just means I get to pick your disguise for the stakeout."

Cocking his head and raising his eyebrows, Katrina couldn't help but laugh at his confusion. "Why do we need a disguise for the stakeout? I thought we could just stand across the street over here and you could get a nice peek at whatever the riddle was leading us to at the store. There is really no need to go closer."

Katrina twiddled her fingers. "No, this is too far away to make out any details. We need to get into the store. We need costumes because I kind of already staked out the stakeout and now the owner will recognize me when I show up. Besides, we have to blend in and be unrecognizable in case we need to go back again. Why do you think we are meeting in front of the costume store? If we can't find what we need, there is also a thrift store at the end of this block, too."

Katrina held up a large bag and pulled a few things from the top out. "I have a few things from home that will work for me, but we need a wig for me and some things for you to pull this off."

Jared still didn't look too sure about the whole idea. "Do you mind if we grab something to eat before we pick out my Inspector Jacques Clouseau outfit?"

Surprised at the old movie reference, Katrina smiled. *Maybe we will get along after all.* "Sure, would you like to go around the corner to the sandwich shop and plan out how we are going to solve this latest riddle?"

They ended up ordering soup and salads and sat down at the café-style tables in the sandwich shop. Katrina pulled a pen out of her purse and drew a diagram of the pet shop on her napkin.

"The store is very full of supplies, and the gentleman who runs the store says that they will pack it with people for their adoption day. We will get there over an hour early, like the riddle says, because the clock is set to an hour early. We need to look busy. Hopefully, something will happen right away. If it doesn't, we need to look like we need to be in there the entire time."

Jared looked skeptical. "What if we see nothing mysterious? How are we going to look busy for an hour? Don't you think we will look odd just standing there looking at our phones?"

Katrina sighed. "Use your imagination. You can pretend that you know nothing of cats and spend the hour asking questions about every little thing. Or you can act like you have a few screws loose and people will avoid you. Hopefully, I'm right and we won't be waiting long."

Katrina pointed to the doorway. "One of us needs to stay pretty close to the entryway in case the person carrying the pet carrier is really quick, like at the park. We don't want to miss him. I think the key to the whole riddle is in the pet carrier. Finding that out is priority one."

Jared asked, "Do we know for sure that this riddle has anything to do with the pet carrier? What if that was just some odd thing that happened at the park? It could have nothing to do with the cat adoptions today. We could just sit across the street and order some coffees."

Katrina's eyebrows furrowed in determination. "You're right, it might have nothing to do with this riddle, but I have a gut feeling it does. After today, we will know for sure. You can't just send me a riddle and expect that I won't get to the bottom of it."

The two of them munched on the last of their sandwiches, and Jared went to take a drink, when out of the blue Katrina asked, "Have you ever played the Would You Rather game?"

Jared nodded his head.

Katrina watched him carefully as she asked. "Would you rather write poetry or have thumb screws used on you?"

Jared's eyes grew large with surprise. Water squirted out of his nose and he started coughing. Katrina hurriedly handed him her napkin.

Chapter Fourteen

The Master of Disguise

Secret Agent Man played through Katrina's head as she and Jared took their places. She wore her red hair tucked under a short black wig and wore large circular glasses. She wore big baggy clothing in layers to make her figure look bigger. The shop owner would never recognize her as Willa's owner now.

Katrina positioned herself near where employees were setting up the pet adoption. That was where she thought she would be most likely to spot a clue. She unhelpfully chatted them up about each cat, asking the most ridiculous and mundane questions that popped into her head. "What is this cat thinking right now?"

The gentleman she addressed looked up at her and shook his head. "Ma'am, I'm not a cat mind reader, but I would say this one might be hungry for his lunch. If you will excuse me, I have a lot of cats to get settled and feed before adoptions start shortly. If you are interested in adopting, I will answer all of your questions then.

Katrina walked up to a woman wiping down mostly empty cages that were built into the wall. "So, does this cat have all nine of his lives still?"

The woman raised her eyebrow. "I'm sorry to tell you, but that's an old wives' tale. Cats only have the same one life that people have."

She got back to work, but Katrina soon interrupted her with another question. The workers became obviously annoyed, but it gave her a brilliant cover. She had a wealth of the oddest questions people asked when they were adopting a cat. "Is this cat scared of cucumbers?"

The woman let out an exasperated sigh. "I'm pretty sure this cat does not have a fear of vegetables, but if you are considering adopting him, head to aisle three to check out the high-quality cat food selection."

Katrina nodded her head and walked toward aisle three while monitoring the employees' activities. Multiple volunteers were entering the building with identical pet carriers. They set them in one area that was a sort of the cat-carrier holding area. The employees were setting up the more visible adoption window cages and emptying the pet carriers one by one. They set the empty pet carriers in another pile that the volunteers took back out to their vans.

It seemed like a simple process, but more and more customers kept coming in and asking the volunteers and employees questions, just as she had done. This distracted them to the point of one volunteer almost taking a full pet carrier back out to the van.

One customer knelt down by the cats, still in the cat carriers, sticking her fingers in the small slats and crooning to their inhabitants. This caused one employee to squeeze behind her, knocking things off of the over-packed shelves in the process. Both individuals were quickly trying to reload the shelves as they brought more cat carriers in the front door and they took more out. It was simply too many people in such a crowded space. It was chaotic. *With so many pet carriers coming and going, how will I spot anything unusual going on?*

Jared was on door duty. He changed out his stylish clothing for old, out-of-style, raggedy clothes they found at Salvation Army. They smelled slightly funny. He wore a large floppy hat that covered his hair and made his features hard to make out. Not that anyone let him get that close to them.

The costume store was mainly a bust. He wouldn't wear the fake glasses and nose she picked out, and she refused to let him wear fake elf ears. Although, she couldn't help but pick up a cat costume that had black spider legs to try on Willa later.

The owner watched Jared like a hawk. She hadn't thought about that when they first picked out the outfit, but at least it kept him from paying any attention to Katrina. He looked at different dog and cat snacks near the front of the store until the owner finally had enough. "Unless you are going to buy something, sir, please step outside."

Jared picked up a candy bar and pulled two wrinkled-up dollar bills out of his pocket. "I think I will have this." He took his change and his candy bar and sat outside the doorway of the store, slowly eating it. The shop owner continued to eye him warily but didn't make him leave with the merchandise he'd recently purchased. He had a bit of time before he had to come up with a new plan.

Katrina was asking more inane cat questions when, at exactly one o'clock, a man walked into the store with a pet crate. Katrina stared at him in shock. It was the same man that adopted Jonesy, the fluffy orange cat, for his daughter this morning!

He walked into the store and nonchalantly set down the pet carrier near a collection of other matching carriers of the cats being adopted today. Katrina watched him out of the corner of her eye, trying not to stare too obviously. He walked around the back of the store, picked up a few items and set them down, as if browsing. Then he slowly took a small bag of cat treats up to the cash register, checked out, and nonchalantly left. His innocent-looking drop-off took him less than five minutes.

Katrina wanted to edge her way over to the pet carriers to see what was inside. *Is he looking for a new home for Jonesy already?* That cat was in her care and was her responsibility to find him a good home. Unfortunately, one employee was still patiently talking to her about if a particular cat passed gas.

Katrina thanked the employee and walked away when an older woman walked into the pet store. She was wearing a shirt very similar to the volunteers, but Katrina hadn't seen her with the others when they were setting up.

She walked straight to the pet carriers. Out of all the identical carriers, she immediately picked up the one that the man who'd adopted Jonesy recently brought in. She moved swiftly toward the door, and Katrina panicked.

I never had time to peek inside!

Katrina moved quickly toward the doorway, but unless she ran up and tackled her, she wouldn't get there in time.

Should I run up and tackle her? That would definitely blow my disguise. It wouldn't be a big deal if this is just an innocent little scavenger hunt, but something tells me there is something more sinister going on here.

As she walked out of the building, Jared came to the rescue. She saw a smile flit across Jared's face as he stuck his foot into the doorway at the last second and tripped the woman. She dropped the pet carrier.

She desperately scrambled to grab it before it hit the sidewalk, but she was too slow. It made a loud thud as the corner of the door hit cement. This knocked the door open and a fluffy orange cat and its cat bed came tumbling out of the carrier.

The cat looked around, shocked for a few moments, and took off like a light down a nearby alleyway. Jared took a grab at the running cat but missed. Then he tried to reach down to help the woman. "I'm terribly sorry, ma'am. Didn't mean to let your cat loose. I'll help you get this picked up, and I will help you find him. Let me make it up to you. We can get some cat treats to tempt him. He couldn't have gotten too far, yet."

The woman glared at Jared and hurriedly reached down for the cat bedding before he could reach it. Oddly, she gently shoved the bed back into the carrier and secured the door before she yelled at Jared, "Watch your feet and stay away from me. I can't believe this shop owner lets vagrants loiter in the doorway."

The owner of the shop made his way over to see what all the commotion was about. He glared at Jared and then held out his hands as he asked the woman, "Is everything all right, ma'am?" When she saw him approaching, the woman stalked off, carefully holding the pet carrier, and not seeming to care that it no longer held a cat.

Chapter Fifteen

Here, Kitty!

"Here, kitty, kitty, kitty!" Jared called out. He laid a few cat treats in front of the pet carrier Katrina had purchased.

Katrina's wig was askew. She waved toward Jared. "Bring the cat carrier over here. I see Jonesy hiding behind the dumpster. Why did you trip her, anyway? You could have injured the innocent cat!"

A little too loudly, Jared answered, "I panicked. You said it was imperative that we see what was in that pet carrier. I did whatever I could to slow her down. I didn't mean to make her drop it. You named the cat already?"

Never taking her eyes off the cat, Katrina's lips firmed. "I just let a man adopt this cat this morning. He was my responsibility, and now this just got personal."

Walking up to her, Jared frowned. "This was just supposed to be a fun little riddle to solve. Our excursion is over, but after we catch this cat, we can still go out for dinner if you want?"

"That little riddle has blown up into something I can't just let go. I take pride in finding the perfect homes for my charges. It's heartbreaking that I was so wrong about that guy. I checked over his application, but everything seemed in order, so I didn't worry about it. Now I'm worried about how many other cats I have released into the wrong hands? I'm sorry, I can't do dinner tonight. I need to get Jonesy settled back at the shelter and need to find him a good home, like I promised him."

Jared gave the pet carrier to Katrina, who placed it on one side of the opening behind the dumpster. Then Jared knelt down on one side while Katrina knelt on the other. They used their bodies to block any exits so the cat couldn't bolt.

Katrina opened a can of cat food. "Come here, Jonesy, look what I have for you. Do you remember me from the shelter? We are going to help you find a new, even better home."

The cat lifted his head, and his eyes followed the food. Katrina set the food inside the pet carrier and then waited patiently. About ten minutes later, the cat slowly walked over to the cat carrier, sniffing and examining the whole thing before stepping inside to eat. Katrina slowly closed the door of the cat carrier and stood up, knocking her forgotten wig onto the ground.

Katrina wiped her baggy shirt over her brow. "Whew, I am glad we caught him. I am going to take Jonesy back to work and get him all settled in. Thank you for your help with the riddle. We wouldn't have gotten Jonesy back if it wasn't for your quick thinking. We now know that the riddles have something to do with that pet carrier getting passed over, but interestingly, the pet inside the cage seems incidental. I'm going to think about this some more."

Jared looked at her, eyes wide. "When will I see you again?"

Katrina smiled. "Let me know if you find another one of those riddles. They are hard to spot with all the information constantly being posted on the Loves Cats forum. Apparently, you have a knack for it. The next step is to get our hands on one of those pet carriers and find out what is really going on here."

Jared raised his eyebrow. "You know, we could just go to dinner like regular people."

Katrina's eyes twinkled. "Dinner is boring compared to uncovering a conspiracy together."

Jared went to scratch his head but looked at their clothing and seemed like he thought better of it when he saw how dirty they were from messing around in the alley. "I mean, realistically, there is probably not anything going on with the pet carriers. The mystery of the cat bed just sounds ridiculous. That was fun, but we should just forget the riddles. Would you be free to go out on my yacht with me this weekend?"

Katrina sighed. "I can't help it. These puzzles have really piqued my curiosity. It will drive me crazy if I don't see it out to the end. Besides, I know cat owners. These people aren't acting like they are excited to bring home a new family member. I think there is something strange going on here, and it's my duty to make sure that I'm finding my cats their forever homes. I'm going to have to pass on the yacht trip at the moment. Maybe after I understand what is really going on."

A bit more curtly, Katrina added, "Don't worry, you don't have to help me. I can do this on my own if you want to back out."

Jared sighed. "No, I don't want you investigating this on your own. I'll keep an eye out for another riddle."

Picking up the cat carrier, Katrina walked back to the bus stop. She had to make it all the way to the other side of town to drop off Jonesy now. She'd been hoping to head home and check on the kittens after their reconnaissance mission. They were looking strong enough that she was planning on doing a supervised visit with Willa.

Oh well, I am only one person.

On the bus ride back to the shelter, she checked the Loves Cats forum. Today was the last day to enter the poetry contest. She never came up with any grand poem, so she made up a cute little limerick to pass the time of her bus ride.

There once was an odd werewolf cat,
Who purred when given a nice pat.
She yowled all night long,
While sharing her song,
Till the neighbor told her to scat.

Katrina knew it wasn't exactly a competition-quality poem, but she still felt better submitting something. It would be really nice if she won a year's supply of cat food. She loved her job, but working at a shelter run mainly by volunteers didn't pay the best.

Before long, she was at the stop nearest to her work. She got off of the bus and took Jonesy inside. It was late in the afternoon. All the volunteers had finished up for the day. Patrick was the only employee there. He was showing a family the dogs they had available for adoption.

Katrina went into the Pet Friends' office and looked up the paperwork from Jonesy's adoption from this morning. She called the number the man gave for himself, Henry Smith. Now that she was looking at it skeptically, it sounded like a fake name. The phone beeped as being disconnected. She tried the references he listed and none of them had heard of a Henry Smith or even someone who'd recently adopted a cat for their daughter.

The family Patrick was working with took a younger dog into one of the adoption playrooms. Once he got them settled, Patrick came over to greet her. "Hey, Katrina! I'm surprised to see you here. I thought you said you were taking the afternoon off for important cat business."

Katrina smiled as she put a cage together with everything that Jonesy would need for the night. "I was taking off for 'impurrtant' cat business. It was so catlike; you wouldn't get it."

Patrick looked away. "Does this have anything to do with that guy you have been talking to online? What was his silly name, Catman?"

Katrina ignored his question as what was really bothering her burst forth. "Do you see this cat? This is Jonesy. Some guy adopted him from me just this morning. Then he had the nerve to pass him off to someone who obviously didn't care about him. I had to bring him back so I could find a new home for him."

Patrick raised his eyebrow at her skeptically, "Ummm... did you steal someone's cat?"

Katrina huffed. "No, some woman abandoned him, and it took me and Jared a long time in a dirty, stinky alley, convincing him to get into this pet carrier."

Scratching at his cheek, Patrick seemed confused as he asked, "Who is Jared? And what are you wearing?"

Oops, I forgot I was still in my baggy clothes and wearing ridiculous accessories. At least I lost the wig at some point.

"Jared is not Pete. Jared is Catman. These clothes are my disguise," Katrina responded. She really was not in the mood to talk to Patrick about Jared right now, so she kept her answer short and vague. She honestly didn't know what to think about him now. *Everything is so complicated now that we met in person.*

Patrick opened his mouth and looked like he was about to ask more questions when the family came out looking for him. They looked like they wanted paperwork to complete the adoption, so Katrina slipped out the door without another word.

It's been too long of a day to deal with the men in my life.

Chapter Sixteen

Without a Paddle

Katrina stood nervously beside the lake in her brand-new bright orange life jacket. She wasn't afraid of water and she wasn't afraid of boats. She feared being in charge of her own watercraft. *I've done nothing like this before. What if I sink it?*

She spotted Patrick gracefully floating in the water toward her. He was in a sleek green kayak that held two holes. Patrick sat in the first portal and a humongous black lab sat in the second one. He held his black head over the water, his nose inches away from touching.

Tied to the back of his kayak by a rope was a second green kayak with only one hole. Patrick towed it along effortlessly.

That doesn't look too bad. What was I worried about?

Patrick pulled his boat up along the shore beside her. Immediately, the dog launched out of the boat into the water. The sopping-wet dog eagerly greeted her, rubbing his wet body against her as he licked her leg.

At first, Katrina took a step back in surprise, but she was out here for Patrick, so she embraced the enthusiasm of the wet mutt. Before long, she was laughing at the dog's delight in being petted as his wet tail wagged so much it thunked against her leg. She was quite wet by the time Patrick made it close enough to the shore to save her.

Patrick lifted himself out of the boat and grabbed the dog by the collar. "Groot, settle down. We get to spend all day with Katrina, get back in the boat." Once the dog settled himself back into his part of the kayak, Patrick turned to her.

"I see you made it. After all the things that kept coming up, I just assumed you didn't want to come. Well, you are in for a treat today. This is one of Groot's and my favorite things to do on a nice sunny day like today. I got everything ready to go down to the boat launch, so we are ready to go."

Patrick stepped into the shallow water to untie the second boat and pulled it up right next to the shore. "I know you love the safety of the pet shelter and your apartment. Are you ready for an adventure today?"

Katrina wasn't completely sure, but she was here and was going to make the best of things. She gingerly tried to step into the boat, but it rocked too aggressively. Patrick used both hands to hold the small boat still while she used his shoulder as a handhold to keep herself steady as she slid her body into the sleeve of the kayak.

Katrina sat low in the boat and panicked. She was so close to the water.

This thing is going to tip over as soon as he lets go. I didn't know my legs could feel claustrophobic in a boat!

Patrick handed her a paddle and lithely hopped into his boat with barely a wobble. "Are you ready to go? You dip one end of the paddle into the water on your right and push. Then you do the same thing on the other side. You go back and forth to go forward. You put more pressure on one side if you want to turn that way. Let me show you."

Patrick dipped each end of his paddle into the water, pushing off. He made it a few yards out into the lake before he came back for her. Katrina put one of her paddles in the water and awkwardly pushed. When she flipped it upside down to push with the other side of the paddle, cold water ran down from the wet paddle onto her arms.

Katrina took another few strokes, making herself soaking wet, and barely made it a few feet toward Patrick. *Why wasn't Patrick getting all wet? My arms are already feeling this. It's a lot harder than it looks.*

They continued on for a while. Patrick would sail ahead and then do a few circles around her while saying encouraging words. Katrina attempted to paddle straight and ended up zigzagging back and forth. It soaked her shirt in no time. *I could see this being relaxing if you were good at it. I'm just very, very bad at it.*

At one point, she dropped her paddle, but to her relief, it floated. *It looks like Patrick picked a foolproof activity. I haven't even tipped my boat!* Groot looked around with his tongue hanging out, living his best life.

After a painstaking forty-five minutes, Patrick stopped her. "You have made incredible progress since you started out. Unfortunately, we will not make it a few miles to that island out there to have a picnic like I originally planned. Would you like to turn back and have a picnic on shore?"

Thankful for the close reprieve, she agreed. Luckily, the current was pushing them toward the shore, so it was a lot faster going back. Katrina bumped into the shoreline, more than ready to get out. Patrick pulled up his boat alongside hers.

Her fingers itched to check her phone, but she'd locked it in her car for safekeeping. *I wonder how my kittens are doing. Do you think*

Catman will forgive my curtness from the other day or did I scare him off? Maybe I can sneak away from our picnic to check on things for a few minutes.

Eagerly, she quickly stood up and attempted to step onto shore. Immediately, the boat rocked and tipped her sideways. Patrick stood quickly in an attempt to catch her. They both landed with a splash. Groot jumped out of the boat, splashing around in the two-foot-deep water. He frolicked around them, joining in on their game.

Patrick looked at her in horror, not sure how she would respond to this catastrophe. *Can I do anything but laugh at this absurd situation?* When Katrina chuckled, Patrick got an enormous smile on his face and laughed too.

Water dripped from Patrick's hair as he asked asked her, "So, what did you think about your first time kayaking?"

Katrina petted the soaking-wet Groot. He then shook himself inches from her face. She shrunk away, but smiled as she answered, "This was a lot more fun than I realized, and Groot is such a good boy. Although, other than being dry, there is one thing that would have made this better... if Groot was a cat."

Chapter Seventeen

Suspicion

Katrina looked suspiciously at the man who wanted to adopt Thackery Binx. She held the black cat to herself, unsure if she wanted to hand him over. "So, what types of plants do you have in your house that Binx would have access to?"

The man gave her an irritated look. "I already told you I only have one little herb garden in my kitchen window with rosemary, basil, and thyme growing in it."

The door jingled as the director of Pet Friends entered. Amy was a short and dark-haired woman. She was nice enough, as long as you did your job well. She liked to be hands-off in her management but wouldn't tolerate when things moved inefficiently.

When Katrina still didn't hand over the cat or even seem to prepare him for travel, the man became more frustrated. He raised his voice as he said, "Look, I already filled out all of your papers. You called all of my references, including the extras that you asked for. I just came in here to get a cat for a bit of companionship. If you don't plan on approving my adoption, stop wasting my time."

Less vehemently, he muttered an afterthought, as if to himself, "I was hoping to get him home before the storm started, but it looks like it's too late for that."

Amy was setting down her things and taking her jacket off in her office when she called out, "Katrina, can you please come to my office?"

Katrina went to Amy's office, still holding Binx. With wide eyes, she peered over the cat. "Yes, what can I do for you?"

Amy raised her eyebrow. "You are usually my best employee at arranging adoptions. You have a genuine gift for finding a good match between our cats and potential owners. Is there a problem out there?"

Katrina shook her head. "No, I was just fully vetting that gentleman out there. He seems like a great fit for Binx, here."

Amy pointed at Binx. "That's great to hear. So, why are you still holding Binx?"

At that point, Patrick came over with one of the adoption boxes. He gave her a small half-smile. "Why don't you let me get Binx ready to go to his new forever home? His new owner doesn't look too pleased with us right now."

He gently pried the cat out of Katrina's hands, secured him in the carry-home box, and walked him over to the man. Katrina watched them go until Amy cleared her throat. "Is everything all right? You don't seem like your normal cheerful self today."

Katrina waved her hand at Amy. "I'm fine. I just wanted to be extra cautious. I just wanted to cross all of my I's and dot all of my T's." She paused for a moment, thinking about what she said. "Or something like that."

Amy eyed her for a few more minutes before going back to working on her computer. "All right, just let me know if you need any help out there."

Quickly, Katrina escaped to the communal cat playroom and sat on the floor. A few cats were napping, others played with toys on the floor. Jonesy came over to her and started rubbing his head against her hand, encouraging her to pet him. She dangled a small stuffed mouse from her hands, and Jonesy put his weight on his hind legs in order to bat at it with both paws.

Patrick came in and sat down beside her. Immediately, three cats came over, begging for attention. "These guys can always tell I am more of a dog person. You would think they are trying to convince me otherwise."

When Katrina didn't answer, Patrick studied her face. "Why were you asking that gentleman all of those questions repeatedly? He looked like a good owner for Binx. I've never seen you act so suspicious before."

Katrina petted Jonesy, contemplating how much she wanted to share. She didn't really want to talk about his distrust of Jared right now. "I was trying to catch that man in a lie. If I ask him the same questions in different ways, I thought I could cross-examine him like they do on the court TV shows. I didn't want Binx to go to someone up to no good, like the man who adopted poor Jonesy."

Patrick sighed. "Jonesy is doing fine. He isn't as emotionally scarred as you seem to be over the situation. Just because we had one unsuccessful adoption, doesn't mean we stop finding homes for these guys. Why don't I leave you here in your happy place to play with your cats for a while? I'm here to talk if you need me, but I'm a volunteer short today and my canine friends don't take a day off from pooping."

Patrick stood up and left. She watched him go, but was feeling more anxious than relaxed. *I should probably get back to work, too. I have so much to catch up on from taking off a few days last week. I'll stay here for just a few more minutes, then I'll get up.* Katrina pulled out her phone and brought up the Loves Cats forum.

She ran through the announcements. Her heart plummeted. *I knew I didn't stand a good chance of winning the poetry contest, but I guess I was still hopeful.* She continued to scroll. She read on until she stopped in shock.

It read: "The recipient of the Loves Cats Poetry Contest requested they remain anonymous. They gave us permission to share that the winner is donating their prize, the year's supply of cat food, to the Pet Friends Animal Shelter. We are so lucky to have such an enthusiastic and good-natured community here. Thank you to everyone who took part. Good luck in next year's poetry competition."

There were several animal shelters in the city, and Pet Friends was one of the smaller organizations. *I am very thankful for the donation, but I wonder why they chose this shelter to donate it to? What a thoughtful gesture.*

Katrina checked her messages, and there was one from Jared. *Looks like I didn't scare him away. After making him dress up in that stinky outfit and stake out suspicious cat owners, I wouldn't have blamed him if he ran away screaming.*

Catman007: Hey, Katrina, I'm sorry for the way we parted the other day. Will you give me another chance?

CuriousKat316: Yes, I'm sorry I was so snippy with you. I was really upset that one of the cats I cared for was involved in some kind of scheme.

Catman007: How about I choose the venue this time? Are you free tomorrow evening? Would you be interested in being my date to an art exhibition I am in?

CuriousKat316: Sure, I didn't know you were an artist. Sounds like fun. Where should I meet up with you?

While Katrina waited for a response, she saw a new message pop up on the general forum with the subject line "Poor Doomed Kittens." She couldn't help but click to read the rest of the message.

It read: On my way home from work, I walked down the rainbow bridge. I heard something like a meow and tiny figures jumping around in a large refrigerator box that was right beside the bank of the river. I think there were kittens in that box. Poor things, there is no easy way to get down to them and all the rain is making the river raise quickly. You guys are amazing, so I thought I would let you guys know in case someone else is braver than me!

Chapter Eighteen

Ghost Ship

Looking down over the edge of the bridge, Katrina chewed on her bottom lip. Through the rain, she saw the box and a few small furry critters jumping around it, but it was impossible to tell if it was really kittens inside.

She shivered. Her raincoat was keeping her mainly dry from the downpour, but it had a way of finding its way into the smallest crevice. The wind on the bridge was making the rain fall at an angle, and her pants were now getting soaked.

Eying the steep hillside beside the bridge, Katrina second-guessed herself. She really didn't want to go down there. If it was a bright sunny day, she could probably maneuver down the hillside, slowly, but safely. Right now, it looked wet, slippery, and dangerous.

Unfortunately, she couldn't bring herself to leave until she got a closer look at that box. She didn't hear any meowing like the person who'd originally spotted them claimed, but if it really was kittens in there, she would do whatever it took to save them. She didn't want any poor defenseless creatures to be swept down the river.

Watching the nearby river slowly rising, she realized she had better hurry. It was already an hour after someone posted about the cardboard box being in danger of being swept away. It was close to the bank of the river, and it looked like it would overflow all too soon. *I have a feeling I'm going to look back on this and remember it as one of the dumber things I've done in life. Well, here goes nothing!*

Walking toward the edge of the slope, Katrina carefully secured her first foot before placing the next one. She slogged her way down the steep incline, holding on to trees when she could reach them for extra support. It was tricky to do while juggling the cat carrier she borrowed from work on her way out the door, but she needed a safe way to transport the kittens after she saved them.

At one point in time, she slipped, but quickly caught herself. With a sigh of relief, she reached the bottom of the gorge and looked back up at the bridge. She'd traveled a respectful distance, but she had made it. *Piece of cake.*

The horrible stench of death filled the air, and she slogged through the muddy grass slowly to make sure she didn't step on anything nasty. If it smelled that badly through all the rain, she couldn't imagine what it would be like on a hot day. She walked up to the box and looked inside. Five small furry bodies looked back at her.

Definitely not kittens! The rodents had short black hair, pale hairless ears and thick rope-like tails. They were surrounding the remains of what appeared to be a dead raccoon, oblivious to the surrounding weather. One rat hissed at her.

Katrina screamed and stepped backwards as another rat left the carcass in the box and scrambled out of a hole in the bottom, right toward her. She slipped and landed right on her behind in the mud.

The rat scurried off under the bridge. Katrina hurriedly picked herself up out of the muck, grabbed the cat carrier, and climbed the muddy cliff as fast as she could before its mates came out to investigate.

She made slow progress, sliding back down a foot for every few feet she made it up the hill. At one point, she hit a particularly slick patch of grass and tumbled backwards, banging her cheek on a rock and dropping the pet carrier. It rolled almost to the bottom of the gorge, and Katrina gave a frustrated groan.

Not caring that there was no one around to hear her, she said aloud, "Why didn't I ask Patrick to come with me? He always has my back. But no. I had to rush off and be the hero!" *On second thought, I probably didn't ask Patrick to come with me because he is too sensible. He would have convinced me not to go down and try to save the... kittens.*

Her cheek stung dreadfully as she made her way back down the hill to grab the carrier. She was in charge of keeping inventory in her section and really didn't want to explain to her boss why this one was missing. *What would I say to her? I went to save some rats that I thought were kittens from an overflowing river? No, thank you. The fewer people who know about this mix-up, the better.*

After another ten minutes of struggling up the steep ridge, she finally made it to the top. She sat down in the mud and let the rain pour down upon her. She was too exhausted and embarrassed to care how wet and muddy she got. *Tonight will be a good night to order in some pizza, snuggle with Willa on the couch, and watch an old movie. I think* Ghost Ship *would be perfect after tonight's adventure.*

Eventually picking herself up, Katrina slowly made her way down the length of the bridge toward the nearest bus stop. She hoped the rain would wash most of the mud off, but she would stand instead of sitting to minimize her dripping mess, anyway. In about a half hour, hopefully, she would get a warm, refreshing shower.

She waited under an overhang near the bus stop, even though she didn't think she could get any wetter. The bus stopped and a plump elderly woman opened the door. Upon spotting Katrina, her mouth dropped. "Ma'am, are you all right? Do you need a hospital? Should I call the police?"

Cocking her head and lifting an eyebrow, Katrina stepped into the bus. "No, I just had a minor accident in the mud. Heading home for a shower now. Thanks." She paid her fare and turned to find an open space to drip in peace.

She caught sight of herself in the interior mirror of the bus. Blood poured down her cheek where it hit on the rock. Mud still covered her hood and jacket, and a twig with a leaf still attached stuck out awkwardly from her hair. She stared at her reflection, that was like looking at a stranger, until the bus started and she had to grab onto the back of a seat to avoid toppling over.

This is the woman Jared wants to go on a fancy date with tomorrow night? Would she even be able to make herself presentable with that nasty gash on her face? *That man doesn't know what he's in for.*

Chapter Nineteen

She's Out of Control

Dancing around her apartment with a dust cloth in hand, she sang along to *Another One Bites the Dust.* Today was Saturday, and she had the day off to do laundry, clean up her apartment, and get ready for her hot date tonight.

Her cheek still smarted from yesterday's adventure, but a small butterfly band-aid on her cheekbone was keeping the gash secured. It bled worse than it looked. Once she got a bath and cleaned it up, all it needed was a small bandage. She hoped Jared didn't ask her how she got it.

Willa walked up to her and brushed against her leg, then walked over to her bedroom door and scraped. Katrina turned off the music. "You have been getting used to the scents of Captain Jackie's kittens for a while now. Do you think you're ready to meet them?"

Willa gave a loud yowl in response and rubbed her head on the palm of Katrina's hand, demanding petting.

"All right, but even though they are getting around and exploring now, you still need to be careful with them. They are just babies."

Sneaking into her bedroom without letting Willa follow was difficult, but she wanted to control this introduction and didn't want any accidents. Willa was a sweet cat and getting along great with Captain Jackie, but she had never seen her with kittens before.

She carefully picked up one of the larger kittens, the gray-and-white one she'd named after the pirate, Francis Drake. Failing at a Spanish accent, she said, "El Draque, it's time for you to meet a landlubber, your Aunt Willa."

She carefully brought the kitten out of her bedroom and knelt down next to Willa with the kitten still in her hand. Willa walked up to the kitten, and the two spent a few moments sniffing noses. Then Willa gave Drake a lick across his face.

Smiling, Katrina sat Drake on the ground in front of Willa but stayed within arm's reach. The kitten gave a small "meow" as he walked up to Willa and brushed along her side. He batted at Willa's tail, causing her to jump away.

Cautiously approaching Drake, she gently batted at the kitten and then took off. The kitten followed, tail held high as he made his way into the unfamiliar territory of the living room. After disappearing behind the couch, the kitten pounced out at Katrina's socks as she walked by.

Katrina raised her hands above her head. "You got me! I'm so glad that you two are having fun!"

Willa brought one of her cat toys over and dropped it in front of the kitten. Drake cocked his head, staring at her, unsure of what she wanted. Willa batted it to Drake, who hit it around the room excitedly as Willa watched. Feeling much more confident, Katrina brought out the rest of the kittens, one by one, for Willa to greet.

Soon, Captain Jackie sat on the couch, purring as she watched her babies explore the new room. They hid behind furniture, chased each other, and tackled one another. Willa enjoyed gently playing with the kittens for a while but eventually climbed onto her cat shelving that was attached to the wall, to take a nap out of reach.

Still monitoring everyone, Katrina attempted to clean her kitchen. She was trying to clear out her refrigerator, but it seemed an impossible task, as the little black kitten she'd named Sam after the pirate Black Sam kept trying to climb into the refrigerator to investigate. After pulling him out of the way for the fifth time, she wiped the cat hair off of her fridge and gave up, shutting the door.

It didn't look like she was going to get much work done around the apartment right now, with so many inquisitive little busybodies getting into trouble. She walked carefully to her bedroom, watching her step. At least she could pick out her outfit for her date tonight.

A thrill washed through Katrina. She was really excited about this afternoon. She really liked Jared. He was handsome and funny and liked cats. He even put up with her disguising him to check out a catnapping hunch.

Moving the hangers in her closet, one by one, she looked through all of her potential outfit options. The one with sleeves was too out of date, the next one was too pink, and then she stopped at a black strapless cocktail dress. Was it too sexy? What vibe did she want for this date?

Jared told her he would pick her up at seven. He had reservations at a fancy restaurant, and then they would head over to an art show that he was featured in. She didn't normally do a lot of fancy, expensive things, but it excited her to get dolled up and go somewhere nice for a change.

She took out the sexy black cocktail dress. What was the point of keeping it in her closet if she wouldn't wear it? Besides, this was also one of the nicest dresses she owned and hoped it would go over well at both dinner and the art show.

She spent the next few hours pampering herself. After a warm Epsom salt bath, exfoliating facial, manicure, and pedicure, she felt tantalizing. For as much effort as she was putting into looking fabulous, Jared better be impressed. She was sure he would look like a ten. Judging from the last few times she met him, he always dressed well. Except, of course, when she made him dress up in those ridiculous old clothes that made him appear to be homeless.

While curling her hair, she heard a crash from the living room. She set the curler down and ran around her apartment in only her lacy bra and underwear, gathering up kittens. She hugged the squirming mischief makers against her mostly bare chest, getting scratched by tiny claws in the process.

She counted and realized she was missing the white one, Thomas. He was pouncing on Willa's head while she looked off into space with eyes narrowed. "Willa, you look done with these guys for now. I'm going to put them away and we will try this tomorrow when everyone is fresh again."

Gently, she scooped him up and brought Thomas to join his siblings, not realizing that Willa had followed her. When she stood up, Willa pounced from her bed into her arms before she knew what was happening. She desperately tried to catch her but ended up landing on the floor with the cat on her lap. "Poor Willa, was I not giving you enough attention? We will have a special snuggle time tomorrow evening after we put the kittens to bed. It will be just the two of us."

Jackie jumped out of the plastic tote, causing it to tip over. It was swiftly becoming too small for her and all the kittens. One by one, the kittens all escaped their containment. As she sat on the floor, she was soon covered in cats and kittens. Petting each of the cats, she said, "Wish me luck, guys. I'm really excited about this date tonight. I hope it goes well. Jared is a handsome man with many dimensions. Imagine me dating an artist!"

A few kittens meowed while Willa laid down on her lap and purred, kneading into the bare skin of her legs. "Ow, that hurts Willa!" She scooped up the cat and set her on the floor, while making sure none of the babies were within stepping distance. "All right, guys, I'll see you in a few hours. It's almost seven now, and I have to finish getting ready."

When she finally had all the kittens secured in her bedroom with Captain Jackie, she went back to the bathroom. At first Willa followed her, swishing her tail as she watched, but when Katrina sprayed perfume, Willa sneezed and left. Katrina was finishing up her hair, still in only her undergarments, when the doorbell rang.

Chapter Twenty

Pretty Woman

Katrina wiggled into her dress and hopped out into the hallway on one foot while trying to strap on her shoes and not trip over Willa. "I'm coming!" she shouted at the door. Finally, she reached the entryway and swiftly swung it wide open.

There stood Jared in a perfectly tailored black suit, holding two dozen red roses, already exceeding her expectations. She smiled at him as she straightened herself up tall. "Welcome, come on in. I just need another minute or two and I'll be ready to go."

Unmoving, he stood there with his mouth hanging open. He stared at her and looked her up and down until she blushed. "Wow, you look amazing!" As if only now remembering he held the flowers, he quickly stuck out the hand holding the roses and gave her a charming half-smile. "Here, I got these for you."

Katrina took them from him and sniffed them. *These must have cost a fortune.* "Aww, thanks. That's so sweet of you. They are beautiful and smell divine." Holding the door, she gestured for him to enter.

"Please come in. I don't want to chase Willa down the hallway in these strappy shoes!"

Stepping inside, he looked around her apartment briefly, taking in all the cat shelving and mouse-shaped toys littering the floor. Willa walked up, meowed loudly, and sniffed at him. Then she rubbed her head against his legs.

"This must be the famous Willa. A pleasure to meet you." He knelt down and gently petted Willa's back.

Smiling at the successful first introduction, Katrina stepped a few feet into the nearby kitchen, got out a glass vase, and filled it with water. As she arranged the flowers, she asked through the open doorway, "It looks like Willa likes you. How many cats do you have?"

Standing up, Jared used one of his arms to scratch the back of his neck. "Oh, I actually don't have any. I think they're fascinating creatures, and I've been enjoying my time trolling the Loves Cats forum. But I don't have one of my own."

Katrina moved to the kitchen doorway and looked at him with her eyebrow raised. "I thought just about everyone on the Loves Cats forum had a cat. Do you want one? I have some kittens in my bedroom that are going to need a good home soon. And if you don't want a kitten, I'm in charge of finding homes for the cats at the local Pet Friends Animal Shelter. I can hook you up with almost any kind of feline friend you would like."

Frowning, she added, "For some reason, we have had a real surplus of cats coming through lately."

Clasping his hands together, he moved from one foot to the next. "I'll think about it. They are delightful companions, but as an artist, I have to paint when the mood hits me, and I sometimes forget to feed myself when I'm working in my studio. I'm just not sure I could properly take care of one right now."

"All right, you know best. If you change your mind, let me know." Gesturing toward the living room, she said, "If you want to come in and sit on the couch, I just need less than five minutes to finish up the last of my makeup, grab my purse, and then I'm all yours for the night."

Katrina hurried down the hallway and looked behind her to see him walk over and glance at the bay window designed for sunbathing cats, and then sit on the edge of the couch, tapping his fingers on his suit pants. *I hope he doesn't get mad if he gets a bit of cat hair on his nice suit.*

Katrina tried to do her makeup swiftly, but a few of the kittens were standing on their hind legs trying to see what she was doing over the top of their containment container, making it tip over again. Captain Jackie swished her tail in sympathy from on top of Katrina's bed but was otherwise no help. Quickly, she secured the box and scooped up all the kittens wandering around her floor.

While hurriedly finishing up her mascara, she heard a loud crash coming from the other side of her apartment. In surprise, her hand jerked, and she accidentally drew a small line of mascara beside her eye. Not sure what was going on, she jumped up, scooped up a last black kitten that hadn't made it into the box with its siblings, and ran into the living room. Jared wasn't there.

Sprinting to the only other common room in her apartment, Katrina looked into her kitchen to see her glass vase broken into a dozen pieces on the floor. Jared was bent over, carefully avoiding the glass, as he picked up the roses.

Words bubbled out of her mouth before she fully took in the scene. "What's going on?" After she spoke, she caught sight of Willa out of the corner of her eye. She was sitting on the counter that used to contain the vase, carefully licking her paws and seemingly disinterested in the mess on the floor.

Jared jumped up and put his hands up in defense. "I just came in here to see what the crash was."

Katrina put one of her hands on her hip and looked at Willa. "Willa! That was not nice. These roses were mine." She picked the cat up and set her outside of the room, then took the flowers from Jared. "Sorry about that. Sometimes Willa gets jealous when someone other than her gets attention."

Without another vase on hand, Katrina took a large plastic Slurpee cup out of her cupboard, filled it with water, and arranged the expensive flowers inside. "There. That will have to do until I can get a new vase for these beauties."

Jared cleaned up the glass. "I can get this cleaned up if you want to finish getting ready, although you already look gorgeous, so I'm ready to go if you are."

She smiled at him, anticipating her night with him more at every moment. "I'll be ready to go in just one more second. I have to finish the cat-eye look I was going for with my mascara."

Chapter Twenty-One

Lady and the Tramp

Walking down the stairs, Katrina felt Jared's eyes on her as he descended a few stairs behind her. Feeling exceptionally attractive tonight, a thrill ran through her body, and she subconsciously walked more silkily than her normal gait.

When they reached the sidewalk, she immediately spotted a two-person red sports car in front of the apartment building. Stopping short, Katrina raised her eyebrows and looked at Jared. While he dressed well, she didn't realize that he was super rich. *I wonder how much he makes on his art? His work must be fantastic to make that much. He definitely isn't a starving artist.*

He opened the car door for her, then quickly jogged around the car to his side. "Ready for dinner?"

Katrina looked over at Jared, their sides touching in the tight interior of the vehicle. "I'm starving! Where are we headed?"

He turned back to her, but the small space made the moment seem intimate. "I made reservations at a new up-and-coming place on the same street as the art show and my studio. You're in for a real treat tonight!"

Revving his engine, Jared took off, heedless of speed limits, toward an area of town that was being revived by young artists and entrepreneurs. He stopped in front of a restaurant that had barely worn brick and sported exposed industrial piping. There was a small sign on the door etched in cursive that read, The Amber House.

There were a few people standing outside laughing and waiting. One young man in a suit opened Katrina's door for her, and Jared got out and handed him the keys. He immediately hopped into the car and drove it off.

Jared held out his arm to Katrina. "This restaurant has one of the best chefs in town. It's quickly becoming one of the hottest spots around, between the food and its chic industrial décor. I hope you like it." They walked in and a maître d' greeted them. "Welcome to The Amber House! Mr. Ackermann, we have your table ready for you. Please, come this way."

Katrina couldn't help turning her head to take in all the décor in this uniquely decorated place. The floors were the original cement of this industrial building, showing age and a few stains, but it was covered with resin to make it smooth. The tables were a beautiful thick wood decorated with only a simple candle in the middle of the table. What stole her breath away was the artistic glass light coverings hanging from the high ceilings. They were bright colors and shaped into impressionistic sculptures.

Watching her look around, Jared told her, "This place is a renovated glass factory. I love how they made something beautiful out of what was an old broken-down building only a year ago. They even kept the spirit of the place."

Jared held out Katrina's chair and sat down himself while the maître d' asked, "Sir, can I get you two a bottle of wine to share?"

"Do you have any of the Screaming Eagle Sauvignon Blanc?" Jared asked.

Nodding his head, the maître d' bowed. "Of course, sir, we ordered it for you after your last request. I'll bring it out immediately."

Raising her eyebrow, she asked, "Do you come here often? Everyone seems to know you well."

Giving a partial grin, Jared pointed to the glass art on the ceiling. "I happen to be very partial to the décor, and since it is just a few blocks away from my studio, yes, I do come here often."

Furrowing her brow, Katrina questioned, "And what exactly is Screaming Eagle wine? I feel like it's a wine that someone would chug at a sports show."

Chuckling, Jared said, "I assure you, this is a fine wine that you wouldn't want to consume in mass quantities. They made it in small batches and a single bottle is worth thousands of dollars."

Katrina stared wide-eyed as a waiter came by, opened a bottle in front of them, and poured each of them a glass. She stared at her glass, looking for gold specks, but didn't see any. Regardless, she was afraid to drink her glass. It was worth more than she made after working all week. Tentatively, she took a sip. It was delicious, but to her unrefined taste buds, it was just as good as a twenty-five-dollar bottle of wine.

The waiter handed them each a menu with no price tags after the dinner options. Looking down the list, Katrina clasped her hands together and bounced her feet. She was getting uncomfortable at just how lavishly expensive this date was already turning out to be. "What are you ordering?"

Jared was staring at her instead of at the menu. What made her feel sexy earlier was now making her feel way out of her depth. She was used to the simpler things in life. Yes, a fancy night out was exciting, but it was a treat for her and seemed like an everyday event for him.

"I usually get the lobster, but tonight I am feeling more like shrimp parmesan. Their homemade alfredo sauce just melts in your mouth."

Setting down her menu, Katrina nodded at him. "That sounds good. I'll get that too."

The waitress came and took their order and they stared at each other awkwardly for a few moments until Katrina finally broke the silence. "So, why don't you tell me a little more about yourself and what I should expect at this art show? I've never been to one before. Have you been an artist long?"

Jared leaned back in his chair. "I have been painting since I was a young boy. I found I had a genuine talent where I could see something and copy it to the exact detail. It's only been the last month or so that I've branched out and tried to sell my own creative art. It's been a bit of a rough start, but I'm confident that with time, people will enjoy my more abstract art just as much as they enjoyed my replicas. At least I hope they do. I feel a renewed passion in my art now that I am doing my own original pieces."

Moving forward in his chair, Jared looked deeply into her eyes and spoke in a sultry voice, "You never know when you will run into your muse."

Their shrimp alfredo came, and it was probably the most delicious pasta dish Katrina had ever tasted. He was right, this place really was a diamond in the rough. If she could afford it, she would love to come back again someday. As they ate, they fell into a comfortable comradeship.

They talked about how Katrina first adopted Willa and laughed over their recent adventure at the cat-adoption event at the pet store. Before long, their bellies were happily full, and they were smiling at one another. No longer worried about awkward idle chitchat, Katrina realized they were having a lovely evening already, and they weren't even at the art show yet.

Standing up and pulling out Katrina's chair for her, Jared asked, "Are you ready to check out some art next? I can't wait to show off my work to you. I really want to know what you think. They got a lot of big names to show at this gallery tonight, and I'm honored to be included. Be ready to be impressed."

Smiling back, Katrina's heart glowed at the wonderful night she was having. "I can't wait to see your art. I'm sure it's amazing!" Soon she would understand the irony of her words.

Chapter Twenty-Two

The Joy of Painting

Comfortably, they walked together a few blocks down the road until they came to a warehouse with the man door opened and a large muscular bouncer up front, holding a clipboard.

When Jared walked up, the man scowled at him. "This is an invitation-only event. Do you have an invitation?"

Head held high, Jared responded, "My name is Jared Ackermann, and your list should tell you I am one of the artists presenting at this exhibit tonight." The man looked down at a clipboard in his hand, then he nodded his head and moved out of the doorway.

Jared smiled at Katrina and held out the crook of his arm. She paused a moment, looking at the intimidating bouncer, and took a deep breath. This was a whole new world to her, but she was getting awfully curious as to what she would find inside. After gently placing her hand on his arm, she let him lead her into the warehouse.

The building itself was dimly lit, but there were dozens of plain white walls spread almost haphazardly throughout the warehouse.

Some were long straight walls, some smaller ones connected to create corners, and one section had three walls connecting to create a large 'U' shape. Paintings and sculptures were decorating every open surface, with bright spotlights focusing on the displays.

There were maybe a hundred people spread throughout the building, all dressed in the finest suits and dresses. She was glad she wore the strapless black dress, but compared to the surrounding women, she still felt underdressed. A few servers walked about the mingling groups handing out hors d'oeuvres and glasses of champagne. Skipping most of the art, Jared led her through the crowd to the back of the building.

On the last wall stood a series of eight paintings where the artist had taken the shape of things and generalized it into the basic shapes of circles, squares, rectangles, and diamonds. *Oh, how sweet. They let a child display some of their art at this show.*

Jared walked up to them excitedly and pointed to one of the paintings. "So, this is my art. What do you think?"

Katrina stared, reading his features carefully to determine if he was joking. This was not what she was expecting from a rich professional painter. She understood abstract art varied greatly from realism, but still...

He stared at her, waiting expectantly.

She spouted off anything she could think of that sounded artsy. "Well, I really like how you captured the true essence of the painting of these pictures by focusing on the more simplified shapes. Here the person was created using diamonds and squares. It makes me feel like there is something special about an ordinary person."

He sidled up to her and gave her a little side hug while they both looked over his work together. "You understand my vision! I'm glad you appreciate the work. Although, I didn't think about the diamonds showing an ordinary person is more than they seem, I will have to use that..." Someone seemed to catch his attention out of the corner of his eye.

He held her hand between his while he arched his brow imploringly. "Do you mind if I leave you for just a few moments? I'd like to hear your thoughts on each of my other works when I come back, but I really need to speak with the organizer of this event for a moment."

She smiled at him as she nodded her head. It would give her time to come up with something nice to say about each piece. "Sure, I'll be fine."

"Thanks, I'll be right back." He took off into a crowd of people and Katrina lost sight of him almost immediately.

She stared at the paintings for about ten minutes, trying to come up with more "artsy" things to say. Two slightly older women came up and stood beside her while examining the paintings. They whispered back and forth to each other, loud enough that Katrina easily caught some of their conversation. "I don't know how he got into this show. His work is something that I could have drawn in a few minutes with some crayons."

The other woman whispered back at her, "I heard he paid his way into this art show..." The two continued to gossip as they walked away. Katrina examined the price tags. It looked like each of the paintings were being sold for under a hundred dollars each. That wasn't bad for an artist just starting with unknown work, but she wondered how he afforded to live so extravagantly. *He must have made a lot with his replica paintings. Or maybe he has family money?* There was still so much she didn't know about him.

Slowly, she moved around to view some of the other artwork and didn't see another price tag under several thousand dollars. Most were around ten thousand or more. The art here was jaw-dropping stunning. She didn't think she would ever see this kind of talent outside of a museum again.

One painter used classical techniques to create a painting and then styled it in different colors akin to pop art. Another covered a metal base with what looked like silly string from a distance, but when you looked at it one way, it appeared in the shape of a man with a dog. When she took a few steps further and looked at it again, the same sculpture looked like a woman with a child.

Along one wall, Katrina noticed a realistic but simplistic ten-foot-long stream going across a long white wall. She almost walked on when she noticed a QR code at one end of the painting and someone else looking at the stream through their phone. She took out her own phone, followed the QR code, and looked on in amazement. They set the painting up with augmented reality.

Little fairies flitted around, hopping from rock to rock. Katrina put her hand out in front of her phone near the stream and one fairy even jumped onto her hand and did a little dance before flying off to join its friends. It was an absolutely stunning mix of art and technology brought together.

It was at this display that Jared found her again. He had two glasses of champagne in his hand and he handed one to her immediately. "Oh, there you are. Sorry, that took me a few more minutes than I intended."

He practically chugged down his own glass. "There's some spirit-crushing critics here that don't understand my work like you do. Would you like to head over to my studio to see where the magic happens?"

Katrina was glad to have any excuse not to give him a full critique of his artwork at the show, so she agreed, "Sure, I'd love to go see it."

They had such a pleasant time at dinner that she really didn't want to end the night on a sour note.

They sat their glasses on a tray one server was carrying around, then exited the show. They followed a line of streetlights about four blocks down when Jared became really excited. "I think you will really like the piece I am currently working on. I really can't wait to hear what you think of it."

He can't wait to hear my thoughts on his work. I really should have seen that coming.

Chapter Twenty-Three

Roxanne

Entering the studio, Katrina was vaguely aware of shelves covered in various paints and brushes, but the first thing that really caught Katrina's attention was the large canvas in the middle of the room. It looked to be a cat with simple black triangles forming the ears and nose, and ovals for the face and body.

Then she took in a few paintings that lined the surrounding walls. One was a framed dollar bill, that upon closer inspection, she realized it was a very detailed painting of a dollar. Another looked like a famous Monet and another was a painted copy of the comic book *Batman, the Dark Knight*.

Jared came up to stand beside her as she circled the room, studying each framed piece of art. "Since I was eight, I have been painting registered replicas of famous artwork. It brought in good money, but I lost the heart for the craft long ago."

This man was an enigma to unravel, but luckily, Curious Kat was up to the task. His detailed replicas of art were in such contrast to the simple shapes of his current work that she felt a piece of the puzzle finally click. It was almost like his current work was rebelling against decades of painstaking detail, as if he was trying desperately to break free from all previous expectations.

When they finished circling the studio, they ended in front of the cat painting in the center of the room. It was easily ten feet wide by ten feet tall, and it sat on an easel on top of a drop cloth. "Your posts on the Loves Cats forum about Willa inspired this latest work. Although, I can't help but think her essence is missing in this one, so I'm still working on it."

Smiling gently, she turned to him. "I'm sure it will thrill Willa to know she is your muse. She loves to be the center of attention."

Jared moved closer to Katrina and gently lifted her chin. "It's not Willa that's my muse. Since I first saw you on that bus, I haven't been able to stop thinking about you. It was you, just being yourself, that finally convinced me to take the leap at making my own art."

He leaned down and tentatively brushed his lips against hers. She felt every nerve tingle where his soft lips touched her own. Dreaming of this moment since before she had met him did not prepare her for the reality of the desire she felt deep within herself. Closing her eyes, she kissed him back more intensely. She felt his well-groomed stubble roughly brush against her cheeks, causing a pleasant contrast of sensation to the pleasure of his soft lips.

He returned her passion with increased fervor, moving his hand to grasp her firmly around the waist of her tight black dress. Things were heating a little too fast for a first date, so Katrina used all of her willpower to break free from the passion clouding her mind. She gave him one last slow parting kiss before laying her head on his chest.

She stood there in his arms for a few minutes, listening to the quick beating of his heart as she tried to slow her own breathing down. With a groan, he pulled away and held her at arm's length. He smiled at her. "If I didn't know any better, I would think you are trying to seduce me in that black dress of yours. Would you like me to get us some more wine?"

She nodded, not trusting her voice. Her fingers brushed against her lips, remembering his touch. Things got dangerously spicy way too fast. She needed to slow things down. This was only their first date, and she hoped there would be many more.

Jared walked to the far side of the studio and pulled a bottle out of a mini fridge. He shouted across the space. "Just give me a few minutes to find us some glasses. I rarely host company here." He disappeared into another room.

She smiled as she watched him go. It looked like he wanted to have a quiet evening with her, and she was looking forward to getting to know him better. She imagined the night in front of them, sitting on that old couch in the corner, laughing and drinking wine until all hours of the night.

Katrina pulled out her phone and opened up the app to the cat-cam in her bedroom. She watched as the kittens pranced about and hid under her bed. She sighed. They were loose again. She heard a soft "meow" and was startled, as she remembered her cat-cam didn't have audio. *How odd. Didn't Jared say he didn't have a cat?* Unable to stop herself, she followed the sound to a small metal door. The door was unlocked, so she opened it and peeked inside.

There was a tall standing-level table with a lamp and a plethora of different art materials. It looked like a passport was haphazardly lying on a pile of papers on one end of the table. On the floor beside the desk was a pile of comic books, stacked high. She took a step forward to enter the room and look around for the sound of a cat.

"Hey," Jared spoke a little too loudly, causing her to jump.

He handed her a coffee mug containing what she presumed was more fancy wine. "I brought us some wine. Sorry about the cup, these were all I could find." He shut the door and stood in front of it as he added, "You don't want to look in there. I use it mainly for storage, and it's full of all kinds of junk and art supplies."

Taking the mug, she looked back at the now-closed door. "I could have sworn I heard a cat in there."

Shrugging, he gulped down his wine almost as fast as the champagne he had earlier. "Sometimes stray cats will find their way in here to catch mice. I try to keep very little food here, but this building is so old that they are always getting in. If I catch it, you will be the first to know."

Unexpectedly, Jared held out his hand and escorted her toward the door. "Well, it's getting pretty late. As much as I would love to pick up where we left off recently, I have some work to finish up tonight for a client of mine, and we still have to walk back to the restaurant to pick up my car. Can I message you about setting up another date?"

Trying to keep her facial expression as nonchalant as she could, she said, "Oh, okay. Yeah, I guess it is getting late, and I should get home. Thanks for a lovely dinner and a night I will always remember."

While disappointed their date was at its end, Katrina felt overwhelmed by her very full night of new experiences, extravagant tastes, and tantalizing kisses. A part of her wanted more of those kisses, but she was feeling exhausted as well. "Yes, another date sounds fun. I just checked my cat-camera a few moments ago, and it looks like those mischievous kittens got loose again, so I need to go anyway. Are you going to come back and work on your cat painting?"

He stared at the painting, frowning for a few minutes before he shook his head. "No, unfortunately, my personal projects don't pay the bills yet. Hopefully, someday I can focus on my art and leave the demands of my clients behind, but sometimes it feels like it's hard to get out of the rut your life is in."

Chapter Twenty-Four

When Harry Met Sally

Staring off into space, Katrina realized her mind had wandered away from a video of an acrobatic cat expertly climbing a tree to get to his owner. After her date with Jared the other day, her mind kept going back to the feel of his lips on hers. The feel of his rough stubble as it accidentally grazed her lips had sent a thrill through her. While at the time she was trying to slow things down, the anticipation of what she would feel if she didn't hold him back kept her body thrumming with excitement.

She really liked him and hoped he liked her too. She was just confused about the way the night had ended. He seemed to enjoy himself and took the time to fetch wine, but then chugged his drink and rushed her out the door. She would have thought that meant he wasn't interested, but he ended the night by asking her out on another date.

Maybe he did just have a lot of work that needed to be caught up on and she should stop trying to read between the lines?

Unfortunately, it had been two days since their fancy date and she hadn't heard a word from him. Maybe he asked her out on another date in pity so he wouldn't have to drive her home after dumping her. She was running every part of their date through her mind to figure out if she did something wrong. Maybe he realized she didn't fit into his world as much as he thought she did. *Since when have I let a guy distract me from my precious cats before?*

She was trying to watch a few funny cat videos, because those normally cheered her up in minutes. Today, she just couldn't focus on them. Instead, she checked for messages from Catman on the Loves Cats forum. She typed out a message to him about what a delightful time she had with him, but then deleted it. She didn't want to sound desperate. He probably wasn't interested in her after all. She choked down a few bites of her tuna sandwich on rye, then put her phone away and went back out to work.

Her lips curved slightly as Patrick walked over to join her. Maybe cute cat videos didn't do the trick, but Patrick always made her feel better. He was the best friend anyone could hope for. He came over and gave her a brief hug.

"Hey, is everything all right? I usually see you smiling up a storm with your cat people and memes on your phone, but today you had your head on your hand and barely ate your lunch. Did one of your cat friends have sharper claws than you realized? Despite what you would like to believe, there are trolls all over the internet, even in cat forums."

Frowning, she looked up at him. "You know me too well. Yes, I'm upset, but not because someone was mean to me. I had a great date on Friday with that guy I was telling you about, Jared/Catman."

A sour look crossed Patrick's face, but he nodded. "Yes, I remember you telling me about that guy who joined your Loves Cats forum because he saw it on your phone when you dropped it on the bus. He didn't seem like the most trustworthy type. What made you decide to go on a date with him?"

Katrina gave an exasperated sigh. "That's not the important part. I thought he was sweet, and we had a fun evening going to an old glass warehouse for dinner..."

Patrick interrupted, "Where did he take you? An old glass factory? You deserve to be treated well on a date. You're amazing, and you're better off without him if he doesn't see that. I think you can do better." For some reason, she wasn't getting the warm feeling from him she was hoping for. She needed his support, not an interrogation.

Placing her hands on his shoulder, she looked him in the eye. "Patrick! He treated me well. We went to a fancy restaurant, drank expensive wine, and saw amazing art at a local exhibit. I'm just upset because I think he's ghosting me now."

Katrina dropped her arms while Patrick looked down at his feet and shuffled them for a bit. "Listen. I'm sorry to hear he hasn't messaged you. He's a fool if he lets you get away. Whatever fancy wines and art shows he tries to woo you with, just make sure he is treating you right and you really care about him. I just want you to be happy."

Hearing her phone beep, she fought the urge to pick it up to see if there was a message from Jared. It took all of her focus, but she didn't want to blow off Patrick, who was just trying to help her. "Thank you, Patrick. You are a fantastic friend."

Looking back up at her, Jared gave her a tentative smile. "Would you like to try out the new escape room in town with me after work tonight to get your mind off of him? There is one that's themed after old movies, and it made me think of you. Unfortunately, they didn't have one about cats, though."

This was the Patrick she adored who knew her so well. An escape room was the perfect idea to get her mind off... Her phone beeped with a notification, totally throwing off her line of thought. She simply had to know if it was Jared.

Smiling broadly at Patrick, she answered him quickly. "Yes! I think an escape room sounds like a lot of fun! That's just what I need. I'll see you after our shifts." Then she held up one finger and pulled out her phone. "If I could just have a minute, I need to get this."

Vaguely aware of Patrick walking away whistling, she quickly opened the Loves Cats forum. There it was. The message she had been worrying over for the last two days.

Catman007: Hey, Katrina, I had such an enjoyable time with you the other night that I wanted to reach out and set up our next date. I was thinking about a fancy dinner and ride on my yacht, but I also spotted another puzzle posted that seemed related to your cat-carrier mystery. What would you prefer to do?

She quickly responded.

CuriousKat316: The boat ride sounds amazing. We should definitely do that sometime, but I have to admit, I'm dying to figure out what is going on with these guys exchanging cats all over town. It just doesn't make any sense. Will you forward the puzzle to me?

Catman007: Sure. Here it is:

My Eastern European Turnips Mix Excellently when Added To Thyme, Haddock, Edamame, and Pork. Understand, you need to Really Puncture each piece of meat to Let Each Piece soak up the seasoning while Laying in the juices. Always add Yolks if substituting Ground meat, but Rabbit will also work in a pinch. Onions should not be added Under any circumstance.

Never Deliver your meal and leave It Near Easily Accessible windows. Serve Turnips atop Pork And beside the Rest of your meal. Keep leftovers refrigerated. We suggest Eating Dessert afterwards! cook for 3:00 hours Past Mixing your ingredients.

CuriousKat316: How do you know it has to do with the cat carriers? This sounds like a really nasty recipe written by someone who doesn't understand grammar.

Catman007: I know it's a different format, but I think they changed it up a bit. I have a gut feeling that this "recipe" is related, but I'm not good at unraveling these clues like you are. Any ideas?

A few hours of puzzling while she worked later, Katrina sent Jared a last message before leaving for the escape room with Patrick.

CuriousKat316: MEET ME AT THE PURPLE PLAYGROUND IN EAST PARK. WED 3:00 PM.

Chapter Twenty-Five

Cube

Looking up at the countdown, Katrina saw they only had fourteen minutes and forty-seven seconds left to escape the room. The room looked like an old movie set, including a small, three-sided fake office. There were two old modeled video cameras pointing at it and lights shining down brightly from the ceiling.

A bead of sweat dropped from her forehead as she dashed around the room, looking for the next clue. Patrick was looking through the drawers of the office desk for the second time, and she saw him get down on his hands and knees to exam the underside of the desk.

She was walking over to the cameras to look through them again. She saw nothing odd through the first camera, no matter where she pointed it. The second camera had a small rectangle drawn on the lens. Moving the camera around, the square fit perfectly over a framed photograph that sat on the desk.

"Hey, I found a clue!" Patrick called out from under the desk. "There was a fake drawer in here with a piece of paper saying, 'You can only beat the odds together.'"

Walking toward the desk, Katrina picked up the frame. "I think I may have found something too." Patrick climbed out from under the desk as she gently took the frame off the photo. They'd taped a small key to the backing behind the photo.

Excitedly, Patrick plucked off the key and held it up to the light to inspect it. "You know, this looks just about the size that would fit into that locked box we found by the doorway."

Face lighting up, she said, "Yeah, you're right! Do you want to do the honors? I feel like we're getting close!"

Rushing to the other side of the room, Katrina looked back at the clock. They were down to five minutes and twenty-two seconds. Where did all that time go so swiftly? How many clues did they have left to uncover?

Unlocking the box exposed two light switches. Patrick hit the first one down and the room turned completely black. Katrina couldn't even see Patrick's outline and he was standing less than a foot from her.

He must have hit the other switch, because one light pointing over the set turned on, but it glowed the dark purple of a black-light. Immediately, two handprints about eight feet apart lit up on the wall of the set.

Katrina took Patrick's hand as they stumbled in the near darkness toward the handprints. She tripped over the lip of the movie set, but Patrick caught her before she ever fell. They each approached a different handprint and tried hitting it with their palms. Nothing happened.

Patrick frowned and pressed on the wall hard enough to make a solid thud. "What do we do with this now? We haven't uncovered any more locked boxes. We must be missing something. Should we mark these spots somehow and examine it with the lights on?"

Holding up her hand to stop him, Katrina stared at her outstretched hand for a second. "There is one clue we haven't used yet. What did you say it was, something about doing things together?"

Nodding his head, he repeated it, "'You can only beat the odds together.'"

Placing one hand on the handprint next to her, Katrina reached her hand out toward Patrick and wiggled her fingers. "I know it's a long shot, but we have less than a minute to figure this out. Take my hand."

Patrick placed his own palm upon the handprint nearest him and grasped Katrina's hand firmly. Katrina looked at the countdown above the door, counting down with only twenty seconds to spare. The door popped open.

Hand still grasping Patrick's, Katrina jumped up and down and gave him a big hug. "I can't believe we did it! We must have made a circuit of some sort with our hands. How clever! This was so much fun. Thanks for making my day!"

Quietly, Patrick responded with an enormous grin on his face. "I'm glad you're happy now. I hated to see you so glum earlier."

Hand in hand, they exited the room. The woman working the counter handed them a sign that said, "We escaped." With a nasally voice, she said, "Use that if you guys want to take a selfie in the room. I'm impressed. That room is designed for four to eight people, but you two beat it. You make a cute couple, and you work well together to boot!"

Blushing, Katrina only now realized she still held his hand. She immediately dropped it and responded, "Oh, we're not together. We have been best friends for a while now." Pointing to her head, she added, "We're just lucky because we are really in sync."

Taking the sign from the woman, Patrick followed her back into the escape room where they posed in front of the movie set and the cameras. Guessing roughly where the handprints were located, they had the receptionist take a picture of the two of them holding hands and grinning with their palms on a blank wall.

Katrina took back her phone and looked through the pictures. "I love this one of us! I'm going to send it to my digital picture frame at home, that way I can remember this fun night forever... or at least until Willa figures out how to knock it off of its hook on the wall and break it."

The two of them walked out the door, but Katrina was enjoying the calm comfort of Patrick's company. "Do you want to get some ice cream before heading home? I mean, unless you have to get back to Groot?"

He gave her a smile that encapsulated his entire face. "My dog will be fine a little longer. I went home during my late lunch to let him out since I knew we were going to do the escape room together. I love the simple sweetness of a good ol' vanilla ice cream cone. Lead the way!"

Pursing her lips as they walked out the door together, Katrina thought for a few moments. "I can't decide if I'm in the mood for vanilla or strawberry today. Maybe I'll splurge and get a double scoop with both!"

Chapter Twenty-Six

Playground

Wednesday came before Katrina knew it. She had to leave work early to be here on time, but she promised to take Patrick's next weekend shift to cover her. She hummed in excitement as she tried to mentally urge the bus to move more quickly, but it didn't.

When she finally got to East Park, Katrina walked a circuit around the purple playground, trying to decide where the best vantage point would be. This time, she wanted to be close enough that she could nonchalantly walk by and see inside the pet crate. Maybe if she was lucky, she would spot something that she'd missed before when she was primarily focused on the cat.

It was two-thirty, and the riddle said that the trade-off would go down at three. She had to pick her spot soon and hope that it was close enough. From her limited experience, they were always prompt.

She looked around for Jared but didn't spot him anywhere, but that meant nothing. While it was a large play area, there were over three dozen children of various ages squealing as they chased each other through the play structure and climbed the rock wall, with parents scattered around as well. On this beautiful day, the area was quite packed.

Finally, Katrina spotted a man lurking behind the bushes in sunglasses and a hat a good distance away from the playground. Could that be Jared? He was terrible at disguises when left to his own devices. She walked toward the bushes, and the man waved for her to come quickly. Yep, it was Jared.

Katrina picked up her pace. "Jared? Why are you all the way over here? This isn't a good place to see anything. Besides, a lone man in the bushes watching the children play is creepy and bound to get the cops called on you."

Jared pursed his lips. "I was trying to be stealthy. Wasn't that why we wore disguises at the pet store? If we hide back here, we can see everything without anyone getting a good look at us."

Crossing her arms, Katrina said, "We were wearing disguises at the pet store so that the owner didn't recognize me as Willa's owner. I wanted to remain anonymous as we looked for clues. I appreciate your enthusiasm, but we really need to get closer. The time for general reconnaissance is over. Now we need to get closer to piece together the clues and find evidence."

Jared raised one eyebrow. "Evidence for what, exactly?"

Rolling her eyes, Katrina pointed back toward the playground. "I'll tell you that when we get close enough to find out!"

"Katrina! Is that you?"

Spinning around, Katrina's eyes grew wide as she spotted Tara walking toward her with a little girl in tow. She gave a tentative smile. *Great.* This wasn't the time for chitchat.

Tara smiled back brightly as the little girl tugged on her arm, eying the playground. "It's so great to run into you. I'm babysitting my niece for the afternoon and we thought we would come to the park to enjoy this beautiful day. What brings you here?"

Katrina glanced at Jared. "I was, ummm... looking for something with my... Jared." She didn't know how else to introduce him. Was he her friend or boyfriend? Neither of them had defined their relationship yet. "It's nice to see you, but we need to keep... searching before the next bus comes." Katrina vaguely gestured toward the playground. She should get a record for the most awkward response. Sarcastically she thought, *I'm not acting suspicious at all.*

Jared walked out from behind the bush. "I'm sorry, honey, but I didn't find that earring you lost on our walk earlier behind this bush either. I'll just have to get you another pair."

Tara glanced back and forth between Katrina and Jared as he held out his hand to shake. "Nice to meet you. I'm Katrina's Jared."

The little girl tugged on Tara's arm harder and whined, "Please, can I go play now?"

Tara glanced down but didn't move. "Sure, sweetie." She shook Jared's hand as she said, "I'm Tara. I volunteer at Katrina's shelter. Since you guys are heading toward the playground too, I can help you look for your earring."

Katrina shook her head. "No, we actually need to search at the bench beyond the playground next. That's where we stopped on our walk."

Tara shrugged. "All right, at least we can walk in the same direction for a bit. Katrina, I have a question I would like to ask you."

Turning toward the playground, Katrina's eyes scanned the area, looking for any signs of suspicious characters or pet carriers. She saw neither. They started walking, and the little girl pulled out of Tara's grip and ran ahead. Jared followed a few paces behind them.

Tara walked close to Katrina and whispered, "So, that Jared guy looks pretty cute. I didn't realize you were dating someone, or at least I had presumed that you had something going on with Patrick."

Quickly interjecting, Katrina said, "No, Patrick is my best friend. There isn't anything romantic between us."

Tara bit her lip and looked at Katrina out of the side of her eye. "That's good to know. So, you wouldn't mind if I asked him out then? It's hard to find such a nice guy that's so good-looking too."

Katrina nodded her head. "Yes, I think you should go for it. I want him to be happy, and he seems shy about asking anyone out. He had a few girlfriends before I met him, but he hasn't even tried to go on a date since I've known him."

They reached the playground and Tara said, "All right. I'll give it a shot then."

Frustrated at not seeing anything related to the riddle, Katrina pulled out her cellphone and looked at the time. It was six minutes after three. She'd missed the trade-off. She was too late and too distracted.

Trying to plaster a fake smile over her frown, Katrina turned toward Tara. "It was great seeing you, and I look forward to seeing you at work later this week. You are by far my best volunteer, and I appreciate everything you do."

Katrina turned toward Jared. "We should probably be off. We spent so much time searching for my earring that I didn't realize how late it was."

Jared looked down at his own phone and winced. "Nice to meet you, Tara. I hope everything goes well with you asking this Patrick guy out."

Katrina elbowed him. "You weren't supposed to be eavesdropping!"

Jared and Katrina walked over to a nearby bench and pretended to look around on the ground for a lost earring. To Katrina's surprise, she found one. She held up a small stud earring with a sparkling paw print on it. She held it up to Jared and laughed. "Look, I found it."

He took it from her and inspected it. "You know... that's actually the perfect earring for you. Now we have to search this entire park for the other one." They laughed as they exited the park, and Jared silently pocketed the earring.

Chapter Twenty-Seven

Rocky Horror Picture Show

What is a cat's favorite condiment? Cat-chup! Katrina tried to keep her chortles to herself as she scrolled through the Loves Cats social media feed. She had a new meme to post for Willa's adoring fans, but first, she wanted to search the depths of this forum to see where Jared kept finding these puzzles that she suspected were a lot more serious than a simple game.

The problem was, she kept getting distracted by every cute kitten she came across. This forum was like a black hole. She could probably spend all day scrolling through its content and not even realize when she got hungry. Pausing at a kitten on a skateboard, she was writing in a comment when she stopped herself. *Focus. You're looking for riddles.*

Looking up from her phone, she peered out the window of her commuter bus in confusion. This wasn't what her normal route home from work looked like. She glimpsed a street sign and groaned. She was so engrossed in cat puns that she missed her stop. Now she was going to have a lot longer walk. *Although, maybe it was worth it, I can't wait to tell someone to wait for a meowment.*

At the next bus stop, Katrina hopped off and looked around, calculating the fastest route home. Before she started walking, she looked at her phone and sent Jared a quick private message on the Loves Cat forum. Now that they had met up a few times, she really should get his phone number from him.

CuriousKat316: Hey, Jared. I was trying to find where you keep finding those cat riddles we are following, but I can't find them anywhere. They must get deleted soon after they post them. Can you show me where you found them so I can keep a lookout?

Catman007: I guess I could. Would you like to get together and I'll show you in person? Are you free tomorrow evening?

Memories of their first date flooded back. Fancy and romantic, bad paintings, and an amazing kiss; it was a night she would never forget. Absentmindedly, she put her fingers to her lips as she remembered his ardent kisses. Yes, she really wanted to see him again, but instead of at a child's playground, maybe this time they could go somewhere a little more romantic and private.

CuriousKat316: Yes, I would love to meet up after work. Do you want to go back to the Amber House, or do you have somewhere else in mind?

Catman007: How about I pick you up at seven and then we decide?

CuriousKat316: Sure, see you then!

Smiling to herself, Katrina walked home. She had a lot of fun last time they were out, but she was more comfortable with low-key activities. Even though Jared seemed to prefer fancier events, he had already shown her he could be flexible. Maybe she should suggest a private picnic, just the two of them? Should she have one already packed when he picked her up, or give him a heads-up so he could dress appropriately?

When she finally made it to her apartment, she did her ninja move, where she swiftly opened her front door, slipped inside and shut it before any of her fur babies could escape. Captain Jackie was there to rub against her shins, but suspiciously, Willa wasn't with her.

Kicking off her shoes like she normally did, Katrina knelt down and petted her one-eyed cat while surveying her living room. Ugh. There were pieces of fluff all over the living room floor, and it looked like it stemmed from a hole in the couch. Drake, the gray-and-white kitten, was still actively batting a piece around the floor.

Looking around for Willa, she frowned when she didn't see her werewolf cat in her normal sunshine perch on the cat window box. Instead, three kittens were curled together in there, napping. She looked over all the cat shelves on the walls and was surprised to see that Mary, the orange-and-white kitten, had learned to navigate them.

Katrina took an unfortunate step toward the kitchen to check for Willa on top of the fridge. Something wet and slimy oozed between her toes. What a mess, less than a few inches away from a perfectly good litter box. She thought she had finished litter box training the kittens, but it looked like someone needed some more practice.

Hopping on one foot, she changed direction and went toward the bathroom. From previous experience, she had learned to keep this room closed when she wasn't home and now that the kittens were older; she kept her bedroom door closed too. Willa had to be in the kitchen. Katrina groaned as she wiped up her foot. She was only an extra fifteen minutes late today!

Finally, making it to the kitchen, Katrina pulled over a chair to see if Willa was hiding on top of the refrigerator in her cat bed. Instead of seeing scraggly black fur, she spotted orange and white fur again. It was Bonney. Apparently, she had learned how to hop from one cat shelf to the next until she made it to the top of the fridge.

She noticed a broken glass lying on her kitchen counter and one of her cupboards ajar. Opening the door, she finally found Willa, scrunched up in the back of the cupboard. Willa gave her a soft meow. Katrina couldn't help but snap a picture of her poor cat to post on the Loves Cats forum, before cleaning up the broken glass and moving the unbroken ones out of the way.

"Aww, my poor Willa. Have the kittens stolen all of your favorite spots to nap? I know you prefer to be the queen mischief maker, but you don't need to worry. They will wean soon, and I'm working on finding them all pleasant homes. This is temporary."

After spending the next hour cleaning up her little apartment and feeding both herself and all the cats, she slumped down on her couch to post the picture of Willa peering out from behind her glass cups. The way the lighting worked, you could only see her two bright yellow eyes and the outline of her face, as if you had to brave some kind of evil thing to get a drink.

Katrina ran her hands down Willa's scraggly coat as she posted the picture. Willa might not be the softest cat to pet, but she sure purred the loudest. After this, Katrina was going to watch the *Rocky Horror Picture Show*. That was what she was in the mood for tonight. Her phone beeped as people commented on Willa's picture. She got everything from "How creepy" to "Are you serving meowjitos?" She smiled. These were her kind of people.

Curiously, she spotted a conversation tab that she had never seen before called *cat delivery*. She clicked on it and, to her surprise, saw a riddle similar to the ones she had solved before. She snapped a picture of the riddle and figured it out.

Five donuts for Henry

Four hot dogs for Carter

Eight street tacos for Miriam

Delivery's complete by 8:30

It was the same dog park where she first spied the cat-carrier exchange. It didn't surprise her when the whole cat-delivery conversation tab disappeared a half-hour later, but instead of sitting down to watch a movie, she started packing. Now she had the perfect idea for her next date with Jared, even though she was sad it wouldn't give them any privacy.

Chapter Twenty-Eight

The Game

Katrina finished placing the last few items into a large cooler bag when she heard knocking. She swung the bag on her shoulder, grabbed a folded blanket, and carefully watched her feet as Bart the kitten batted at her toes as she made her way to unlock the door. There stood Jared, looking sharp, even though she told him to dress casually for a picnic.

He wore a short-sleeved collared shirt and khaki shorts. She was only in capris and a V-neck T-shirt. Now that she saw him, she wished she had a cute little sundress to throw on before they left. If she kept seeing him, she would definitely need to upgrade her wardrobe.

Carefully making sure that all of her roommates were safe inside, Katrina shut the door to her apartment, locked it, and greeted Jared with a grin. He held out a small jewelry box, and Katrina's eyes went wide. He popped it open, and inside were two little paw-print earrings that sparkled even more than the one she found and held outside in the sun. *They can't be diamonds, can they?*

Katrina took the box to examine them more closely. "Aww, that is so sweet but way too generous. I can't accept these."

Shrugging, Jared said, "If you don't like them, I can give them away, but I had them custom made for you, so I can't return them."

After eying them for a moment more, Katrina took her own earrings out. "Well, if you can't return them, I guess I may as well wear them." She popped the new paw-print earrings in and showed off her ears to Jared.

Jared pointed to the small cooler and blanket she'd brought out into the hallway with her. "What's that?"

Katrina's face lit up. "Oh! There is another riddle. Are you ready to go on a picnic at the dog park? I figured if we pretend we are on a date right by the bench they are meeting, we can..."

Jared interrupted her and looked down at his shoes. "Actually, Katrina, I was thinking about it on the way over here, and I don't really want to follow the riddles anymore. It was fun, but I really like you, and I don't want you to get involved in anything shady. Let's do anything else. I'll take you to the most expensive restaurant in town, Blues. It may normally take months to get a reservation, but I have an understanding with them."

Katrina cocked her head. "We aren't dressed for Blues, but I thought you were having fun going on our little adventures. Why do you want to stop when we are so close to figuring this out? Besides, weren't you the one who sent them to me in the first place, letting me know something strange was going on? I know in the pit of my stomach that more is going on here than people simply getting a new pet. I'm dying to sort this out. If you don't want to come, that's fine. We can do something else, but I simply can't stop now. I'll continue following these riddles by myself until I get to the bottom of it if I need to."

Rubbing the back of his neck, Patrick grimaced. "No, I was having fun. I just don't want you getting in over your head. Maybe these people are up to something illegal, and they will get dangerously angry at us for meddling? We can go, but let's sit away from the bench. You can do a bit of surveillance, and we can have the pleasant picnic you prepared for us."

Enthusiasm drained, Katrina looked up at him. "Are you sure you want to go? I don't want to make you go with me. I can sort this out on my own."

Jared gave her a smile, but Katrina feared he might have forced it. "Yes, I appreciate that you made us a picnic. Let's go."

After loading into Jared's expensive vehicle, they drove to the dog park on Miriam Street and parked. They walked to the Henry Carter bench, but instead of setting up their picnic close by, Jared found a spot under a tree a good distance away. Katrina laid out the blanket, and Jared sat down beside her. They still had a half-hour until the cat drop was supposed to happen, so they got out their picnic. Katrina didn't take her eyes off the bench where the next cat pass-off was supposed to happen. She would not miss anything this time.

Jared fidgeted a lot and kept looking around the park. He barely ate a bite of his food. Katrina frowned. "Is everything all right? You didn't have to come."

Standing up, Jared brushed off his pants. "No, I'm happy to come. It's a beautiful day, but I think I'm going to walk over to the bathroom. If I don't make it back in time for the tradeoff, just stay here on the blanket."

Katrina furrowed her brow as Jared walked off. Something was wrong. He definitely wasn't acting like the relaxed and charming man she was getting to know. Maybe she was focusing on these riddles and potential catnappers too much. She decided she wouldn't bring it up again and instead ask him more about himself. Maybe he would tell her about the comic books she saw lying around in his studio. She realized she still knew very little about Jared other than he was rich and painted for a living. She really liked him, so she would make it her mission to fix this.

While Jared was still gone, she spotted a man in a business suit walking by with a pet carrier. She thought it might even be the same guy she saw when she tracked down the first riddle. He stopped at the same bench the previous drop-off occurred, set down the carrier, and stood looking around for a few moments. She watched him tap his foot while he looked at his watch. He got out a phone, talked to someone, and then walked off, leaving the carrier beside the bench.

Katrina couldn't believe her luck. She knew she should probably stay on the blanket like Jared suggested, but she was dying to know why these people would cart around cats, make up riddles, and trade them all around town. She hopped up off the blanket and quickly made her way to the carrier.

Inside lay a fat Persian that stared back at her. Its fur was matted in places, but it looked like it had a collar. Katrina carefully partially opened the cat carrier to see if there was identification on the collar, when someone tapped her shoulder and cleared their throat.

In surprise, Katrina looked up, but the Persian cat pushed out of the opening and sprinted toward the nearest bush. Katrina lunged toward the cat. "Oh, no! Come back here! Don't run away."

Unfortunately, it was too quick for her, and she soon lost sight of it. She quickly got to her feet to chase after the cat when the man behind her brusquely said, "Excuse me, ma'am, but you are going to have to come with me."

Katrina stopped in her tracks and focused on the policeman beside her. He pulled out a pair of cuffs as he continued talking. "This gentleman here would like to press charges against you for stealing private property, and I need to take you down to the station to ask you a few questions."

Her jaw dropped as the policeman gently but firmly put each of her hands into cuffs. She'd never been arrested before and didn't know what to expect. Would she have a record now? Was she going to jail? "Sir, I'm sorry. I shouldn't have touched this cat crate, but I stole nothing. There is something really strange going on. I think these cats are being smuggled around the city for some reason, and I was just trying to get to the bottom of it."

The policeman raised one of his eyebrows, and Katrina noticed a name tag that read *Bruce Smith*. "Well, that's the first I've heard that one. Why don't you tell me all about it after we get you processed? There are enough strays around here that I can't imagine why anyone would need to smuggle more into town. It's not like cats are illegal."

Once he secured her, he turned around with his mouth open as if to speak to someone. He stood for a few moments with his eyebrows furrowed as he looked around. "That's strange. He was right here. Ma'am, maybe you will get lucky today and you won't have charges pressed against you, but I am still going to take you in. Maybe he ran off to catch his cat, or maybe he headed straight to the station."

Officer Bruce picked up the empty pet carrier, briefly glanced inside, and closed it up. From her vantage point, all Katrina could see was a normal cat bed inside. She wasn't expecting the cat to be sleeping on gold or anything, but she was missing something. Things just didn't add up.

He held the carrier in one hand while he directed her toward the squad car with the other. Katrina looked around desperately for Jared, but he was nowhere to be seen. It was only after she was in the police car that the shock wore off enough that she remembered her purse with her phone and wallet that she left at their picnic spot.

Katrina used her sweetest voice to say, “Please, Officer, I forgot my things close to where you stopped me at the park. I’ll go with you, but can I go pick them up?”

The policeman shook his head as he pulled his car out into traffic. “I’m sorry, ma’am, but we will have to send another officer to pick up your things. Right now, you are in police custody.”

Chapter Twenty-Nine

Birdman of Alcatraz

Katrina spent hours alone in a holding cell, was processed, questioned, and finally released. She was exhausted when later that night, they finally told her she was free to go. She didn't know what happened to the cat carrier, and the police said they couldn't find her things as she described them in the park. Jared must have taken them. But what would he think happened to her? What would he think when he found out they'd arrested her for doing exactly what he warned her not to do?

This was officially the worst date ever.

Picking up the phone the officers offered her, Katrina didn't want her family to know where she spent the night, so she called the only other phone number she had memorized, Patrick. To her relief, Patrick answered almost immediately. "Hello?"

"Hey, Patrick, it's Katrina. I don't have my phone or my wallet right now, and I was hoping you could come and pick me up and take me home?"

She heard Patrick's voice raise as he asked hurriedly, peppering her with questions, "At this time of night, you're not home with your cats? Are you all right? What happened? Where are you? I'll come right away."

Katrina scrunched up her face as she answered. "I'm all right, but I'm actually at the police station. It's kind of a funny story, but I'm not up to telling it right now. I'm pretty exhausted."

"I'll be right there," Patrick responded succinctly, and hung up. She respected his friendship and hoped he wouldn't be mad at her or think her foolish when she told him about the riddles. The whole reason she hadn't mentioned them yet was because he was so negative about Jared, and she feared he would try to dissuade her from following the clues. He would try to convince her to let it go.

The problem was that the questions gnawed at her while she slept and stayed in the peripheral of her mind as she went about her workday. She was just too curious to let it go, especially when it came to her precious cats.

She sat on a bench and waited, hugging herself as she got chilled from the cold, sterile police building. This was not where she intended to spend her day when she dressed for her picnic on a bright, sunny day. She watched officers come and go, bringing in big scary-looking delinquents. She wasn't cut out for places like this. All she wanted was to be home cuddling with her cats on the couch.

About twenty minutes later, Patrick rushed through the door, looking around wildly. Katrina stood up and walked over to him with a tentative smile. He rushed over, enveloped her in a firm embrace, and then looked her over as if to reassure himself that she was all right. "What happened?"

Katrina looked around as her cheeks brightened. "Do you mind if we walk while we talk? No one came to press charges, so I can leave."

A little too loudly, Patrick said, "Press charges! What happened?"

Taking him by the elbow, she led him outside and told him about the riddles on the Loves Cats forum and how she and Jared were having fun investigating it... until tonight. "I didn't mean to let the cat in the carrier go at the park. I just cracked the door so I could look for a phone number on the collar. No matter how curious I was, I would not steal it or anything."

They passed a fast-food restaurant that had a sign that it was open twenty-four hours a day. Katrina stopped. "Do you mind if we stop in to get something to eat? I'm starving and I never got to finish my picnic. I don't have my wallet right now, but I can pay you back tomorrow."

Patrick opened the door to the restaurant and held it for Katrina to walk through. "I'll pick it up, but it will cost you some more answers. Why would you let Jared talk you into this? That guy always seemed a bit squirrelly to me."

Katrina looked at her feet. "Actually, he didn't want to go on the picnic, and was afraid I was getting in over my head. I'm the one who pushed it because I really wanted to sort this out. I still think there is something going on, but I'm thinking the cats are just the cover. If the police didn't have that cat carrier in custody, maybe I could search it to find out..."

Patrick spun her toward him and looked down into her eyes. "Katrina, didn't you learn anything from tonight? It's probably just some innocent cat breeders buying and selling around town, and if it's something more sinister than that, you don't want to get mixed up with it. Please let this whole thing go."

Scrunching her lips together, Katrina stayed silent. Sure, it sounded easy enough to just let it go, but if everything was legitimate, why bother with the riddles and sly handoffs? Her curiosity nagged at her brain. She would be more cautious, but she couldn't just let it go. She felt like she was on the verge of figuring the whole puzzle out, and if she pushed just a bit more, the entire mystery would be revealed to her.

Patrick stood there waiting for her response. She was too tired to argue with him, and her stomach growled at the smell of burgers only a few feet away from them. A half-truth wouldn't be lying to him and would get her a burger faster. "I'm sorry. I appreciate that you're worried about me, and I won't touch any more cat carriers that don't belong to me or the shelter."

She felt Patrick let out a large sigh and then he let her go. "I can't convince you to stay away from Jared too, can I? That's kind of fishy that he took off right before you got arrested."

Katrina shook her head. "No, he just had to go to the bathroom and probably does not know what happened to me. If he will forgive me for ditching him on our date, I would like to see where things go with him."

Patrick furrowed his brow but let the subject drop. "I'm going to get myself a milkshake. I feel I deserve it after tonight. What do you want?"

With her mouth watering, Katrina said, "I'll have a milkshake and all the burgers."

That night, Patrick walked her up to her apartment. Luckily, he had a copy of her key from when he was helping with the newborn kittens. Before she could finish unlocking her door, her neighbor, Mrs. Danglehauser, rushed over.

She held Katrina's purse, small cooler, and blanket in her hands and handed them over. "Oh, Katrina! I'm so glad to see you. A young man came by hours ago looking for you and seemed quite upset. He asked me to return this to you."

She looked over at Patrick and then looked back at Katrina, wide-eyed. "Oh, I'm sorry if I made problems for you, deary. I probably shouldn't have mentioned him in front of your gentleman here." She stood as if waiting to see if Katrina would deny or confirm having multiple "gentleman callers" showing up at her doorstep in a single night.

Katrina gave a loud, exhausted sigh. "Mrs. Danglehauser, I appreciate you bringing me my things, but you don't have to worry. Patrick here is just a friend. I hope you have a good night."

Digging around in her purse, Katrina was relieved to see everything in place, including her phone and keys. She swiftly opened her door, slid inside, and became immediately bombarded with cats. She heard Patrick laugh out loud at the onslaught of kittens behind her. "You would have thought these guys were starving to death!"

"Yep, it's a few hours past their normal dinner time. They think they are starving." Katrina knelt, gave everyone around her legs attention, and snuggled Willa as long as she would tolerate it while hungry. She filled the food dishes and got fresh water before digging her phone out of her purse.

There were multiple frantic messages from Jared.

Catman007: Katrina, where did you go?

Catman007: I'm going to eat your sandwich if you don't come back to our picnic soon, lol.

Catman007: Katrina, are you there? You didn't approach the men with the cat carriers, did you?

Catman007: Please, answer me to let me know you're all right!

She was too tired to explain everything that had happened tonight, so she sent back a quick reply. Looking over into her living room, she saw Patrick holding up a cat toy that was a baton with a feather at the end of a string. He was swinging it around as a kitten tried to pounce and catch it. He didn't look like he wanted to go anywhere, so she would need to kick him out if she wanted to go to sleep.

CuriousKat316: I'm fine and home now. Thanks for dropping off my things. I had a brief run-in with the police, but I'll explain everything tomorrow.

Chapter Thirty

Homeward Bound

A week later, Katrina sat on the bus stop bench. A new bus paused, loaded, and drove away while she watched. After everyone was gone, she looked into the cat carrier beside her and the two amber eyes of a male calico kitten blinked back at her. "I'm going to miss you, Cal. You are such a sweet boy and special. You're a one-out-of-thousands rarity, and I'll probably never meet another just like you." Male calicos were a very rare genetic anomaly that she would probably never see again, even though she worked with cats every day.

The cat purred and rubbed his face against the grates on the front of the crate holding him. Katrina stuck her fingers between the grates and petted him. "I think you will be happy, boy. I checked out everything I could about these people except looking through their trash, and I think they're legit."

She leaned closer to the crate and whispered, "After the crazy cat-nappers that I have been trying to unravel, I would have gone through their garbage for you too if I didn't think the police would start getting suspicious about me."

Standing up, Katrina stretched her legs. They were sore from sitting on the bench for so long. She crossed the busy street and walked less than a block down the street, still within easy view of the bus station. After climbing a few stairs, Katrina took a deep breath, and she knocked on the door.

A middle-aged woman answered and then quickly yelled behind her. "The cat! Laney, come here. Your new kitty's here!" She heard the pitter-patter of tiny feet as a small girl, about seven years old with pigtails, scampered down the hallway. She peered around her mother, trying to get a look inside the pet carrier.

Reflexively, Katrina took a partial step backwards. "Yes, ma'am. Are you Mrs. Whitney? All that we have left is the home inspection, and this little fella is all yours."

The woman smiled and moved out of the way so Katrina could enter. "Yes, we're the Whitneys. This is little Laney. She is so excited to get a kitten of her very own."

Katrina couldn't help as a shiver ran down her back as she fought back the suspicion that was clawing at her mind. Just how far were these mischievous cat villains willing to go? They wouldn't go through the effort of putting together an entire fake family to get a single cat when there were so many strays they could just pick up. Right?

No, that would be ridiculous. This is a wonderful home for Cal.

A soft meow came from the crate, and the little girl looked into it. "Aww. You're so cute! I'm going to call you Colors. Do you want to come to my bedroom, Colors?"

Mrs. Whitney laid a hand on the little girl's shoulder. "Be patient Laney, Colors will get to see your room, but not yet. First, we have to let this nice lady see that we have a suitable home ready for Colors, and then we have to get him used to his new home slowly, so he doesn't get scared. Would you like me to take you around, Miss..."

"My name's Katrina. Yes, let's get this tour finished. You have a beautiful home, Mrs. Whitney." The little girl smiled at her, and Katrina couldn't help but return her infectious joy. She remembered getting her first cat at about the same age. The cat ended up being her childhood friend and confidant through many trials. A cat was a great pet.

They walked through the house, and while everything looked clean and in order, they already had more treats and toys purchased than any single cat could use. A small part of her wanted to find some reason that she needed to keep Cal. Her small apartment was overrun with cats right now and she needed to find the kittens homes, but she was sure going to miss them.

After she finished her tour, Katrina knelt down in front of the pet carrier, and Cal purred at the sight of her. She opened the crate slightly and gave him a pet on his belly. "You be a good boy and take care of your new family, okay?"

She turned to the little girl that was hopping from foot to foot and gave her a sad half-smile. She came over and gave Katrina a squeezing hug. "Thank you so much for bringing me my new kitty. Don't worry, I will take good care of Colors. He will be my best friend forever and ever."

"I think he will be very happy living here and being your best friend. Goodbye, Mrs. Whitney. Goodbye, Laney. Goodbye, Colors." With that, Katrina left, not wanting to embarrass herself any further. She sighed as she walked back to the bus stop. One kitten successfully placed with his forever family, but so many more to go. While she found homes for cats every day in her job, she had to admit that she was going a bit overboard in verifying everything before leaving these little guys, but she would never forgive herself if she accidentally gave her babies to this cat-trafficking ring.

Everyone she mentioned cat-trafficking to laughed at her. They either told her to drop it because she was over her head or let it go because it was a ridiculous notion. In her gut, she felt there was something there. Katrina stopped mentioning it to both Patrick and Jared, but she couldn't bring herself to drop it entirely.

Her bus came, and she found a seat. As normal, she got out her phone and logged onto the Loves Cats forum and immediately looked for new messages from Jared. Nothing.

After she reassured him she was fine after being arrested for a little misunderstanding, he was mysteriously phone silent. They barely exchanged a few messages, and he hadn't asked her out again. He claimed he was really busy with work right now because someone lost some of the replica paintings he made, but while she really liked him, it was feeling like she was getting the cold shoulder.

She rode home enjoying a few cat jokes. She now couldn't wait to ask Patrick at work tomorrow why it was hard to trust cats. He would roll his eyes when she said they have many tall *tails*. She briefly considered messaging Jared "What made the cat upgrade his phone? He wanted to finally get pawtrait mode," but she let it go. She liked him but didn't want to push it if he was no longer interested in her.

To her surprise, right before she got home, a new riddle in her cat-smuggling mystery popped up. She was determined to solve this thing once and for all, even if it meant doing it by herself.

Chapter Thirty-One

CATS!

The next morning, Katrina set up some teen volunteers to socialize her cat charges in the large common area cat room. She wished she had known offering to play with kittens could be counted as volunteer hours when she was a teen, although they would also learn how to clean and disinfect the cat cages next, so it wasn't all fun and games.

With a few free moments to herself, she pulled out her phone to find the riddle she was trying to solve. She may have been physically at the animal shelter, but her mind was so close to solving this riddle that she could taste it. She read the message. If it wasn't in the same secret tab, she probably would have scrolled right past it. It appeared as nothing out of the ordinary on a cat-centric social media site.

Pussycat, pussycat, what did you do on Friday?I've been to London's gardens to visit the Queen.Pussycat, pussycat, why wait until 9 PM?A frightened little mouse will meet me there.

While this poem had a bit more of an ominous tone, her mind read the short poem with a cadence that reminded her of a nursery rhyme she'd heard as a child. Katrina did a quick search and came up with the original words to the nursery rhyme:

Pussycat, pussycat, where have you been?

I've been to London to visit the Queen.

Pussycat, pussycat, what did you do there?

I frightened a little mouse under her chair.

She compared the adapted version of the nursery rhyme to the original, but before she could finish, Patrick came over. Katrina quickly stuffed her phone into her pocket. If he caught wind of another riddle, he would definitely try to dissuade her from going. Looking up, she caught a broad smile crossing his face when their eyes met. "Hey, Katrina. How are things? Are you all recovered from your crazy weekend away from home?"

Katrina rolled her eyes. "Ha-ha. Next time I need a vacation, I think I'll book better accommodations than the local jail. You sure seem chipper today. What's up?"

Patrick pulled two tickets out of his pocket. "I won two free tickets to see the live performance of *Cats the Musical*. I knew you would be the perfect person to take with me."

Her heart beat faster in excitement. That was a show she'd wanted to see live since she was a little girl. "Yes, of course! Thank you so much. When are we going?"

Tapping the tickets against his palm, he said, "You can pick out your favorite pair of cat ears, because the show is this upcoming Friday."

Katrina's face fell. The nursery rhyme puzzle mentioned this Friday. Should she go to the musical with Patrick or finally solve this riddle once and for all? Her curiosity would only continue to eat at her if she didn't wrap up her investigation in some way. "Oh, Patrick, I'm sorry, but I have other plans on Friday. You should ask Tara. She hangs onto your every word, and I have a feeling she's been dying for you to ask her out."

Patrick shoved the tickets back into his pocket and looked at his shoes. "You're going out with Jared, aren't you? You're right, maybe it would be a good excuse to ask Tara on a date, never mind." Head downcast, he turned to walk away.

"Oh, Patrick. I'm sorry," she whispered to his retreating figure. It wasn't like he was big into theater or anything. It surprised her he was taking it so hard that she couldn't go, but he was her best friend. She would make it up to him as soon as she solved this.

That evening, Katrina walked into her apartment and started in shock at the tiny white footprints covering her apartment. Willa came to greet her at the door, completely covered in a white powder. She picked up the cat despite the powder covering her clothing and walked into the kitchen. A box of pancake mix lay tipped over on the ground and spread across the floor. After Willa knocked it off the counter, she must have rolled in it.

It must have happened relatively recently because Captain Jackie seemed oblivious as she lay in the sunshine of the cat window and only one kitten had flour on their paws that Katrina could wipe off with a towel relatively easily.

Willa was a different story. Katrina sat Willa down in the pile of flour and snapped her picture. Willa looked like she was trying to dress up as a ghost for Halloween. She was sure she could make a meme out of that. She cleaned up the worst parts of the mess and then took Willa for a dreaded bath. After many angry yowls and scratches, she towel-dried her feline friend.

Willa's scraggly black-and-gray hair stood on end, and Katrina giggled and took another picture. "Willa, you make the rangiest-looking puffball I have ever seen! I think I will label this: Me trying to get ready for an important meeting on a Monday."

After everyone finished eating and was settled, Katrina logged onto the Loves Cats forum to post her new memes. She saw a thread called "Cat-urday" She scrolled through the thread of owners with their feline pets, and she couldn't help but post a picture of her with Willa and Captain Jackie. She was posting the meme of Willa and putting in all of her associated hashtags so fans could easily find it, when a message from Jared came through. Excitement rushed through her.

Catman007: Hey, Katrina! Sorry I have been so busy with work. I am finally getting my head above water and was wondering if you wanted to get together this Friday night after work? Do you want to go out on my yacht?

She took a few moments to respond. Why did everyone want to do something on Friday night when there was a perfectly good Thursday right before it? She was excited to go out with Jared again and was glad he was still interested, but she remembered how weird he was getting about the riddles. She should probably do her investigating on her own. A little white lie and she could do it all. Patrick invited her to go with him, even though she told him she was busy.

CuriousKat316: I would love to go out on your yacht with you, but unfortunately, my friend Patrick invited me to see the musical *Cats* with him on Friday night. Can we schedule something for Saturday?

Catman007: Sure, it's a date. Want to meet up at 2:00? We could take my yacht out for an afternoon spin and have dinner out on the water. Have fun at the musical.

CuriousKat316: That sounds like so much fun. I'll be there.

Perfect. Now she could stay up late Friday completing the last of her sleuthing, sleep in, and still have enough time to look good for an afternoon yacht ride! She couldn't wait for this weekend; things were starting to really go her way.

Chapter Thirty-Two

Catnapped!

Katrina moved around the park called London's Gardens as stealthily as she could. She didn't know exactly where the cat pass-off would happen, so she wore all black and was trying to stick to the shadows as she looked around.

Tonight, she planned on following them back to their car. Maybe if she got a license plate number, the police would find it belonged to someone with a lot of prior arrests and take her seriously. If she was really lucky, maybe the people would get on a bus and she could monitor them as they rode to their place of business. Possibly, another cat would be left unattended. Katrina knew she didn't have enough information to fully flesh out her plan, but there were too many unknowns to make a solid plan. She would just have to follow her curiosity to see what hard evidence she could uncover.

Looking around, Katrina tried to make out what hid in the shadows. This place was beautiful in the daytime, but looked rather ominous in the darkness. She tried to picture the bright flowers, shimmering water fountains, and well-manicured bushes that were currently obscured. Normally, there were children laughing and smelling the flowers, mothers pushing their strollers, and couples walking down perfectly-cared-for paths hand in hand. She was having a hard time imagining anything beyond the surrounding lumps.

She felt like she was in an immersive inkblot test where everything looked monstrous and only felt better when she found a box bush whose shape was reminiscent of a cat. After only about ten minutes of skulking around, she saw the outline of a person standing beside a pathway.

She stood stock-still, waiting to see where this person would go. The person never moved, and no one came to meet them. What was going on here? After a while, Katrina's muscles were stiffening from standing still so long… and her phone rang. It was Patrick.

Katrina's eyes grew wide as she quickly turned off her phone and dove behind the nearest bush. The person still didn't move, and she got suspicious. Slowly, one step at a time, she approached… the bush. Her heart beat steadily in her chest as she reached out and felt the scratchiness of twigs covered in tiny leaves.

She walked around to the front of the bush and realized she'd just wasted who knew how long staring at the manicured creation of a bear standing on two legs. Covering her face with her hand, Katrina groaned. What if she missed the trade-off again?

Worrying more about speed than stealth, Katrina moved from the shadows of one large bush to the next as fast as she could. This park wasn't an enormous one, but she'd wasted so much time on that fake bear and there was still a lot of ground she hadn't checked. The other hand-offs lasted only a few moments. Even if she missed the official trade, maybe she could still find one of them leaving that she could follow out of here. She had to know what was going on.

She spotted a light bouncing around the path not too far to her right. *Found him!* More carefully, she started moving toward the light, hoping this would not end like her recent bear hunt. She got close enough to see a man flashing his light around as if searching for something. He had a phone up to his ear and was saying something. She stayed hidden behind the trunk of a large tree, peering out only enough to keep an eye on him.

After a while, he moved down the path. Katrina shadowed him, keeping her distance and trying to walk as quietly as she could. He didn't have a pet carrier in his hands, so this was probably the guy who dropped it off. She had hoped to follow the journey of the cat, but she would just have to take what she could get and follow this guy instead.

To her surprise, she felt a strong arm wrap around her waist as a second man reached around her with a sweet-smelling rag in his hand. She struggled to extract herself and run, but that arm held her in place and she couldn't go anywhere. In a last-ditch effort to avoid the rag covering her mouth, Katrina jerked her head backwards and heard a nasty sounding crunch as her head slammed into his nose.

The arm holding the rag fell as the man cursed and bent over, reaching for his face. Like a wildcat, Katrina kicked backwards with all her might and scratched at the arm holding her. She only landed a grazing blow, but his arm around her waist loosened, regardless.

Katrina broke free and ran with all her might back the way she came, toward the exit of the park. She would be safe in the little convenience store beside the bus stop, right? It was hard to see in the pitch dark, and she felt herself tripping over uneven ground, but she knew she had to keep going. She fell, panting, and heard the crack of someone stepping on a branch not too far behind her. A flash of light hit off a tree not far to her right.

She quickly got to her feet and kept going. Before long, she could see the expanse of the dark parking lot in front of her and panicked. She still had a decent distance to go to the nearest bus stop, and she didn't know how far anyone was behind her. She was too frightened to stop and look.

Unused to running so much, Katrina got a stitch in side. She knew she was slowing down, but she tried to force herself to ignore it and keep going. She was at the edge of the park when she felt someone dive at her from behind, holding her legs immobilized. He yelled behind him, "Got her!" Then he pulled out a rag that smelled sweet, like the one she'd escaped only moments earlier.

He held it over her face. Fear jolted down her spine as she tried to scream, but she couldn't get out more than a muffle as they held her in place. Too soon, the darkness she saw in front of her turned pitch black as she slumped in a loss of consciousness.

Katrina woke with a headache and tried to remember what happened. Her body felt like it was in one piece, although the ground was cold and hard. She felt something soft brush against her face.

Her eyes popped open, and she looked around, trying to comprehend what she saw. She had to be hallucinating. Maybe this was all just a bad dream. She was in a large cage on a cement floor… surrounded by cats.

Chapter Thirty-Three

Nine Lives

A few hours later, Katrina sat on the ground, petting a friendly gray tabby that insisted on sitting in her lap. If this was a hallucination, it was a pretty powerful one. There were six cats in the cage with her total, and while none of them were in dire straits, she could see a few rib bones, indicating that they needed to be fed more often.

The cage was made of thick metal bars that were too strong for her to bend and narrow enough that none of the cats could escape. There was enough head room that she only had to hunch a little while sitting down and covered about six square feet of the ground. There was a metal lock keeping the door closed, but without a key, she was stuck.

One cat had on a collar with an address near her apartment in the city, and another she was pretty sure someone had adopted from her very own shelter. Two of the cats eyed her suspiciously and hissed anytime she moved. Either they were strays or treated poorly by humans, but she didn't know which. The last two seemed normal, friendly cats, but she'd never seen them before today.

She was worried about her poor babies at home. She fed them before she left on her adventure, but who knew how long she was unconscious? Daylight streamed through a nearby glass-block window. At the minimum, they had missed their breakfast, and she had no way of contacting anyone to get to them. *Willa and Jackie must be starving.*

She looked around the room, but there wasn't much else in this musty basement but the cage she was in. She did not know what she'd gotten herself into and had no idea how to get out of it. Maybe she needed to worry about herself. Unlike the cats of tall tales, she didn't have nine lives.

After a while, a man came stomping down the stairs. He had tape over his nose and bandages covering one of his arms. He held a plastic plate with two pieces of pizza on it, with cheese that had congealed from sitting out. "Here. I brought you something to eat until we get our instructions on what to do with you. What are you, a reporter? Trying to blackmail us? Why have you been nosing about?"

Softly, Katrina said, "I'm sorry, I'm not a reporter and I'm not here to blackmail you. Believe me, I didn't mean to cause you trouble. I simply wanted to know what you were doing passing pet crates off all around town. I see now that it was none of my business. You can let me out and no one will be the wiser."

He glowered at her. "We are the good guys. We were just helping people out with getting passports, and now we have to deal with you. I didn't sign up to kill nobody."

He folded the paper plate in half, capturing the pizza inside, and slid it through the bars. "Eat up. This might be your last meal."

The cats surrounded Katrina, trying to get close to the plate, and meowed loudly. Suddenly, everything clicked into place. She knew she should probably stay silent, but she was dying to know if her assumptions were correct. *I hope that my future grave doesn't say* curiosity *killed the Kat*. "You had fake passports hidden in the bedding under the cat carriers, didn't you?"

The man nodded his head and turned to walk back up the stairs. He stopped with one foot on the bottom step. "You're too smart for your own good. You should have stayed out of this. We were making good money, and no one knew any better. The police even gave over a million dollars' worth of passports back to one of my men when they accidentally took in one of our carriers by mistake. We all moaned when our supplier had this brilliant idea of hiding them in pet carriers. I mean, who wants to deal with cats? But it worked marvelously... until now." The stairs creaked as he ascended.

Katrina called out, "Wait! Do you have something to feed the cats?" The man didn't return and didn't answer, so she looked around at her cell mates. "It looks like we're sharing." She threw little bits of cheese around the cage to ensure that each cat got something to eat and gave herself space to consume the cold, hard crust. Forcing herself to choke it down, Katrina didn't know when or if she would get a next meal. She had come a long way from that fancy dinner at the Amber House.

A while later, she heard voices speaking loudly upstairs and a lot of walking. Things eventually settled down until she heard two sets of feet walking down the stairs to the basement. *Is this dinner or the end?*

The injured man who'd brought her the pizza earlier came into view first. This time, he was carrying a bowl of cat food in one hand and a small Chinese takeout box in the other. "Here, we had some leftover rice I thought you might want." It was crazy what would make your mouth salivate when you were starving.

A few seconds later, a second man appeared in a crisp, collared button-down shirt. He smiled at the man holding her captive and jingled a small cat toy in the air. "Thanks for letting me deliver my treat to the kitties despite your 'complication.' I'm sure you guys will have it all sorted out soon."

Katrina's jaw dropped and stared at them, speechless. It was none other than Jared.

Chapter Thirty-Four

Betrayal

While the man delivered the food, Jared held his finger up to his mouth behind the man's back, signaling that she should be quiet. *What is he up to?* He obviously knew this guy and was part of this passport-smuggling ring. The question was, was he now a friend or foe?

The big man turned to Jared. "You know it will not please the boss that you stopped by. The whole reason we are using these cats is to make sure we do not jeopardize the business. Everyone is supposed to stay in their own part of the supply chain, so make sure you don't come back."

Jared nodded his head. "Don't worry, I'm here on behalf of Hugo. You know how valuable I am. He has me checking in on the entire supply chain to look for any holes." He raised a single eyebrow at the man. "I'll be sure to report back *every* soft spot I find in your part of the operation."

The man pointed at the cage and stammered a bit as he spoke. "Well, you can ignore the complication that's in the cage right now. It was our competent surveillance that allowed us to catch her spying on us. You can be sure to tell Hugo that we will take care of her later tonight, and there won't be an issue. Your 'mules' are in the cage with her, healthy as can be. Happy?"

Jared looked at the small stuffed mouse in his hand. "Yes, it looks like you guys have everything under control here. I just brought a little something to keep your cats busy. You know how I have a soft spot for them."

Jared patted the man on the back and grinned at him. "You know what, Jimmy? Let's have a drink before I go home, to celebrate a successful surprise inspection. You and Tom can help me with the bottle of whiskey I have in my car, right?" He grimaced. "I have to head out of town to check in on deliveries. It's part of our joint operation tomorrow, but that can wait for another day, right?"

Jimmy's shoulders relaxed as the one side of his lips twitched into a momentary grin. "Sure, I think we can do that. I think a bit of liquid courage will go a long way for what we have planned tonight." He moved back from the cage, and Jared threw in the cat toy before quickly retreating upstairs. "Have fun, kitties." *That bastard! He didn't even acknowledge me!*

Katrina yelled at the retreating figure, "Hey! Come back here!" He didn't even pause on the stairs and soon he was gone, along with her hope. She'd trusted him, and before this, she was wondering if she was falling for him. This betrayal felt like a knife through the heart. Would she ever be able to trust again? Would she survive long enough to try?

Clenching her teeth, she was so angry that at first, she didn't realize the cats were enthusiastically pouncing and batting at the toy mouse. *It must have catnip in it.* Katrina was taking deep breaths to calm herself down when she realized that oddly, every once in a while, the toy mouse would make a metallic ping noise when it hit the floor on its side.

Risking her fingers, Katrina quickly reached out and grabbed the toy as the cats surrounded her, meowing and pawing at her, trying to get it back. She turned the small toy over and saw the stitching was loose on one side. Using her long fingernails, Katrina reached in and pulled out a small key from amongst the catnip in the mouse.

She tossed the mouse back at the cats and turned the key this way and that, as if unable to comprehend that she was truly holding it. Moving closer to the door of her cage, Katrina put the key in and turned. The lock immediately popped open.

Opening the cage, Katrina crawled out and let the cats free to roam the basement. She started checking all the basement windows, looking for a place to escape, but they were high and made of glass blocks, with no openings. Maybe if she had a tool of some kind she could get through them, but this basement was pretty empty other than the cage she was recently in.

It looked like she would have to head up the basement stairs. While Jared had helped facilitate her escape, it sounded like there were two men that she would have to get past. Then she didn't know how long it would take her to get to a safe place. It was still light outside, but she couldn't hear the constant noise of traffic that she was used to in the city.

Placing a foot on the bottom stair, Katrina tried to come up with a plan. Should she charge up the stairs and hope there was a door nearby or try to be sneaky? Using every ounce of stealth she possessed, Katrina tried to ascend the stairs quickly and quietly. Unfortunately, they were so old and worn that almost every step creaked, making her wince. It didn't help that she had a cat hopping around her feet on the stairs, too.

By the time she reached the top stair, her heart was beating so hard that she hoped it couldn't be heard on the other side of the door. She slowly turned the door's knob before opening it only an inch and peering through the crack.

To her surprise, the door swung open the rest of the way, causing her to grab onto the handrail to avoid falling down the stairs. The cat at her feet took off like a bullet into the house, and Katrina made a run for it. Hoping against hope, she headed toward an outside door.

Chapter Thirty-Five

On the Run

Katrina felt an arm grab her shoulder, and she immediately struggled to shrug it off and keep running. She calmed down when she heard Jared's voice behind her, whispering loudly, "Hey, settle down. I just got those two big goons to sleep, and I was coming to help you with that nasty cage. Come on, let's get out of here, and then we can talk."

"They're asleep?" Katrina tried to look around her, but couldn't see the two men from the top of the stairs.

"I roofied their whiskey. We have some time, but we really shouldn't hang around here." He gently tugged on her arm for emphasis.

Pausing for a moment, Katrina followed him. He was mixed up in all of this somehow, but at least he seemed like he was on her side. He gave her a key and was helping her escape. They walked outside as the sun was setting. Katrina looked around at the old farmhouse she was trapped in, trying to remember every detail that would help with a police investigation.

The wooden house needed a new paint job but looked otherwise structurally fine. It had a wraparound porch with a swing that she would have thought of as charming if it didn't hide a smuggling operation. Around the house were tall cornstalks in all directions, as far as one could see. There looked to be a dilapidated shed in one corner of the property, but otherwise, there were no other buildings in sight.

Jared led them to a small old car, and Katrina cocked her head in confusion but followed him into the car. She didn't want to risk being trapped here while she yapped. "Where is your fancy sports car?"

He sat down in the driver's seat and started up the engine, then gave her a sad smile that didn't reach his eyes. "When I heard through the grapevine that a woman was captured trying to spy on this operation, I tried to get ahold of you. Then, when you didn't show up for our date on my yacht, I traded in my beauty for this clunky junk. I figured I would need to be inconspicuous after I rescued you."

Katrina laid a hand on his. "Thank you for saving me, but what exactly are you mixed up in? If you're in trouble, talk to the police."

He squeezed her hand back. "I wish it were that easy, Kat. You know how I'm really good at creating painting replicas? Well, I can make copies of other things too, using all sorts of materials that make it unidentifiable from the originals. I have been supplying these guys with illegal passports for years and making good money off it. There is nothing for me with the police other than jail time."

They drove down the road, passing many farms. Katrina tried to spot some of the road signs, but she had no idea where she was. "Why would you send me those riddles and pretend like you were helping me figure them out when you knew everything? You were part of it all along?"

Jared let go of her hand and ran it through his hair. "So, I have spent a rather obsessive part of my life perfecting my skills at making replicas and reading comic books for fun. I have gone out on dates here and there, but I've never really been in a serious relationship before. Until I met you, I was mostly content. Then one day my car broke down and it forced me to ride a bus. I was stunned by this beautiful, intriguing redhead, and I just had to know more about you. When I picked up your phone, I saw you were on the Loves Cats forum, so I went home and made an account on there and introduced myself to you."

Katrina raised an eyebrow at him. "Couldn't you have just asked me out on a date like a normal person?"

Pursing his lips, Jared said, "It was a lot less intimidating to talk to you online, and it gave me time to test the waters and make sure you wouldn't flat-out tell me no. At first, the riddles seemed like a fun way to get your attention, and I loved dressing up with you and getting to know you. The more I got to know you, the more I wanted to better myself. After watching you forge your own path, I wanted to do more than just replicate things. I wanted to make my own art. You made me want to be a better man, and I tried doing my own thing. It wasn't long after I took you to my studio that I tried to get out of this whole passport business. I wanted out so I could have a genuine relationship with you without secrets and lies."

Jared pulled the car off the side of the road and turned it off. He turned toward her, looking her directly in the eyes. "It turns out Hugo wouldn't let me get out. Without me, he had no supplier, and his entire operation collapsed. He would lose millions of dollars in revenue a month, and he wasn't about to let that happen without a fight. He threatened me, and I realized I was foolish to think about this as a fun game. I tried to stop sending you the riddles and dissuade you from following up with your sleuthing. You have no idea how much I really care about you. I didn't want you to get hurt. I'm sorry I got you mixed up in all of this."

Katrina's eyes grew round. "We can still fix this. Do you have your cell phone? Let's call the police, and I'm sure they will cut you some kind of deal if you turn in Hugo and the other people in this smuggler ring. They will know you got me out. We have to get help."

Jared leaned forward and gave Katrina a small kiss on the forehead. "You are going to get help and tell the police everything, but I can't risk spending my life in jail. I'm not made for that kind of life."

A tear ran down Katrina's cheek. "What do you mean? What exactly are you going to do?"

Jared used one of his fingers to wipe away the tear. "I'm leaving. I can't tell you where I'm going, but it will be somewhere that I can finish figuring out who I am and how I want to live my life. Please know how much I care for you because I don't know where the future will take me. You're an amazing woman, and I'm not sure that I will ever stop thinking about you."

Jared pointed to the corn that ran parallel to the road. "Do you see that corn? I want you to walk a row or two hidden inside the rows of stalks until you get to a diner. It's about a mile and a half that way. When you get there, call the police and tell them everything."

Jared seemed like he was trying to give her a small smile, but it was so forced it looked more like a grimace. "By the time the police get to you, I should be long gone. Goodbye, Katrina."

Chapter Thirty-Six

Waitress

Emotions roiled in Katrina's stomach as she moved swiftly through the corn. It was dark outside, other than a partial moon shining from the sky. The rows were so narrow that she needed to tilt her body slightly as she moved, but Katrina could still move at a decent speed.

She didn't know how far she had to go, but she was already so tired and exhausted from her adventures of the last day. She couldn't imagine a life where she never saw Jared again. It felt like things were just beginning between them, and now it was over.

She spotted a light not far in front of her, so she picked up her speed. Seeing Delilah's Diner, she stepped out of the last stalks of corn and crossed the short parking lot before she pushed open the door.

Inside the slightly dirty fifties-style diner, one lone man sat at the counter drinking a cup of coffee with a piece of partially eaten pie in front of him. A clock above the counter read nine-seventeen. This complete nightmare had lasted less than twenty-four hours.

She walked up to a small counter and an older woman in a well-worn uniform walked over to her. Her name tag read Barb. The woman looked her up and down, causing Katrina to look at herself. She was still wearing the black outfit she put on for being stealthy at the London's Gardens, only now she was covered in a coating of thick cat hair. She felt her head and pulled out a leaf she'd accumulated from her run through the corn.

She looked up at the woman. "I need a phone. I need to call the police. Now."

Barb's eyebrows rose. "Are you all right, honey? There is a phone right beside the cash register you are free to use. Can I get you something to drink?"

Katrina followed her over to the cash register and picked up the phone. "A glass of water would be amazing. Thank you. I'm sorry, I don't have the money to get anything else."

After calling the police and explaining where she was over the phone, she hung up. Barb brought over a glass of water and a large piece of cherry pie. "This is on the house, honey. Why don't you find yourself a seat while you wait?"

Katrina picked up the water and downed it before replying, "Thank you so much. That is so sweet. Do you mind if I make one more call?"

The woman took the glass and refilled it. "You help yourself, hon. It seems like you have been through quite a trial."

Katrina dialed Patrick. She felt a wash of relief just hearing his friendly voice. "Hello?"

She almost sobbed her response, "Patrick! It's so good to hear your voice. I hate to ask you this, but would you be able to do me a favor and pick me up again?"

Patrick chuckled. "Sure, let me know where you are. What has Curious Kat gotten into now?" She was glad he wasn't mad at her anymore for missing the theater with him.

After taking a deep breath, Katrina asked, "Well, first I need you to go to my apartment and feed my cats. You are the only one who has a key to get in, and I have not fed them since last night."

All playfulness gone, Katrina could detect a note of alarm in Patrick's voice. "What happened? Where are you? Your cats will be fine for a few more hours; I'm coming to get you now."

Katrina was so tired that for once she didn't argue. Hopefully, the police wouldn't be too long and she would be home cuddling her babies soon. With the way she was feeling right now, she might never leave her apartment again. "I'm at a small diner in the country outside of town called Delilah's Diner."

She heard Patrick's voice say firmly, "Don't leave that spot. I'll look it up and will be there as fast as I can." Then he hung up.

Katrina picked up her pie and water and found an empty booth to slump into. She picked up her fork, thinking about how thankful she was for Barb's unfettered kindness. *I wonder if Barb's in the market to adopt a kitten?* Before she could take a single bite, two policemen walked through the door and spotted her. Her night had just begun.

The police peppered her with questions and called in backup to meet them at the farmhouse she described. Tomorrow, they expected her to come back to the station to answer more questions, and while they said she could go home, they also made sure she knew not to leave the general area.

She was only alone for a few minutes when Patrick rushed through the door. He spotted her and immediately rushed over. He scooted into the booth beside her and pulled her into an embrace. Katrina happily rested her weary head upon his brawny chest.

He held her tight as he spoke. "Oh, Katrina. You can't keep scaring me like this. Are you all right? Does this have to do with Jared and those puzzles? I thought we agreed you would stay away from that cat-smuggling ring you were talking about."

Eventually, Katrina pulled back to look at Patrick better. "Yes, it had to do with the puzzles, but I didn't exactly agree to drop the whole thing. I just told you I wouldn't touch any cat carriers that didn't belong to me or the shelter, and I didn't."

Patrick let out a gigantic sigh. "I just worry about you. Seeing you at work is the highlight of my day. I don't know what I would do if something happened to you."

Taking another gulp of water, Katrina said, "I'm sorry to worry you, but I just had to know what was going on. Did you know that I uncovered a passport-forgery business? They were using cats as a cover while they secretly transported them in the bedding of pet carriers. Jared was their forger. He's gone now."

Patrick's eyes grew wider as she talked, but softened when she talked about Jared. "I'm sorry. I know you really liked him. Are you ready for me to take you home to your precious cats?"

Katrina laid her head back against the booth. "Oh, yes. I'm never leaving home again. I'm going to become that crazy cat lady who never leaves the house and is discovered years later buried underneath hundreds of cats."

Patrick started to move out of the booth but paused and gave her another side hug, this time accompanied by a half-smile. "I hate to tell you this, but you already are that crazy cat lady."

After moving out of the booth, Katrina looked up into Patrick's eyes. There was a slight quiver in her voice as she spoke. "It's been a really crazy day. Do you mind staying over on the couch? I would just feel safer having someone there."

Patrick wrapped his arms around her and pulled her head against his chest. "Of course. I will always be there for you when you need me, no matter how much trouble you get yourself into."

Chapter Thirty-Seven

Swipe Right

Two weeks later, Katrina woke up to find Willa lying on her face and Captain Jackie curled up behind her knees. Her apartment was quiet now that all the kittens were adopted, but these two were acting very clingy and meowed their displeasure if she was even a little late with their mealtimes.

She moved Willa off of her face, but laid in bed gently petting her fur baby. After answering many questions for the police, the FBI got involved, and she had to answer them all over again. They had her under surveillance in case Jared tried to get in touch with her, but he and his yacht were gone. With a faked passport, he could be anywhere.

It was only in the past few days that authorities finally seemed to be leaving her alone. She took a deep breath to revel in her relative solitude. It felt so nice to get back to normal life where she could focus on her cats.

Without getting out of bed, she picked up her phone and logged onto the Loves Cats forum. She had gone internet silent since the incident two weeks ago. She had a few messages asking for Willa updates, but mostly, everyone's cat lives had moved on. There were more cat memes, jokes, and puns. In a way, it was sad that the group she spent so much energy and time devoted to didn't even realize when her world collapsed.

She spotted an unread text. Patrick. He was always there when she needed him. Stable and strong, like a rock. She never had to worry about him doing illegal anything.

Patrick: Are you sure you still want to go back to the farm today? I can go do it for you, if you want. I can't imagine going back there after what you have been through.

Katrina: No, I want to go. I'll be fine. Thanks for coming with me.

Patrick: Okay, I'll be there to pick you up at 11.

Katrina: Great, see you then.

Captain Jackie stood up and stretched, arching her back and extending her claws. Then she meowed while rubbing her face against Katrina's prone form. Willa stood up and curled on her chest. Looking her straight in the face, she gave a soft meow.

Gently moving her cats to the side, Katrina got up. "All right, all right. I'm getting up. Don't worry, I won't forget breakfast."

Katrina finished setting up a medium-sized live trap, and Patrick walked over with a bag of cat treats. He had two feline friends in tow. "I can't believe the police said they couldn't find any signs of cats around here anymore. All I needed was a little bribery and the two came running. Although I see no sign of the other four you mentioned anywhere in the house."

He handed her the bag of treats, and Katrina scooped up each of the cats and secured them into a pet carrier before handing them both their reward. "Well, the police wouldn't let us in here for almost two weeks. The other four cats could be hiding or they could have taken off. We can come back tomorrow to check on these live traps and hopefully we will catch one of the wilder ones if they are still around."

When Katrina first told him about her intentions of coming back to the house to find homes for her fellow captives, she had insisted that she could handle it by herself. Now that she was here, she was happy Patrick tagged along. She still had nightmares about that cage in the basement, and the entire house was making her feel very uneasy. He had searched the inside while she set up a few live traps on the outside. She never even had to enter the front door.

Katrina picked up one of the pet carriers and loaded it into the back of Patrick's car. "Do you mind if we stop by that diner for lunch? I would like to thank that waitress, Barb, for being so kind to me."

Patrick hopped into his car. "Sure, whatever you need. I'm starving; I could really go for a burger."

While they were driving, Patrick quietly asked, "You haven't brought him up, and I understand if you don't want to talk about him, but I just wanted to know. Are you all right with Jared being gone?"

Katrina was quiet for a while as she examined her own feelings. "I am definitely upset with the way things ended, but honestly, we weren't dating long and our relationship was just beginning. In retrospect, I think Jared had some things to work out that would have eventually doomed a relationship anyway. I've eaten a lot of ice cream and watched the *Rocky Horror Picture Show* almost a dozen times, but I think I'm doing all right."

She gave him a grin as the diner came into view. "I even thought up a great idea. A project is just what I need to throw myself into right now."

They pulled into the diner's parking lot, but before they went in, Patrick held her hands in his own and looked her in the eyes. "You know you can talk to me about anything, right?"

Katrina smiled at him. "I know. I can't tell you how much I appreciate how you have been there for me through all of this. Thank you. Now, are you ready to try the most delicious cherry pie you have ever eaten?"

Patrick laughed. "I can't wait."

They walked up to the door and their hands accidentally brushed up against each other. After a moment, Patrick grasped her hand as they walked in together. Katrina smiled up at him. "So, I had this idea for an app. Do you want to hear it?"

Patrick nodded as they walked up to the counter. "Sure, what's your idea?"

Barb came to the counter. "Barb, I wanted to thank you so much for your kindness to me when I was having the worst day of my life."

Barb pulled out a pen and pad of paper. "I was happy to help, honey. Can I get you anything?"

Katrina looked over at Patrick, and he nodded his head as she ordered, "Can we have two burgers and two cherry pies with tea for dessert?"

They found the booth that Katrina had sat in two weeks ago. Barb brought over their drinks, and Patrick leaned forward with his arms crossed on the table. "So, what is your big idea and how can I help? It will be good to see you excited about something again."

Giving her biggest Cheshire grin, she crossed her arms and leaned toward Patrick, too. "I was hoping you would offer to help. So, I was thinking we could make a dating app, but instead of finding humans that match you, the app would pair you with the perfect cat. What do you think? We could put a handsome or funny picture of a cat with a profile, and then people could swipe right if they are interested in meeting that cat or swipe left if it wouldn't be a good match."

"I think it's a fantastic idea." He got out his phone and scrolled through his contacts. "In fact, I have a buddy who makes apps I can put you in touch with."

"Nice. I can't wait to come up with profiles for my shelter friends. I mean, who wouldn't want to adopt Josie, a rockstar, or Kitty Purry who is a singer and songwriter?"

Raising his eyebrows, Patrick asked, "Things are never boring in your life, are they?"

Katrina shook her head. "No, not really, but do you really want them to be?"

Chapter Thirty-Eight

The Emperor's New Clothes

A month later, Katrina sat contentedly in the darkness on a large flannel blanket. Patrick sat beside her, pouring them both a cup of hot chocolate from a thermos. They sat on top of a hill about an hour's drive away from the city.

Life had gotten back to normal. She went to work, played with her cats, posted on the Loves Cats forum, and hung out with her best friend, Patrick. Tonight, he was nice enough to invite her to an amateur stargazing event. There were a few other couples also in attendance. They briefly greeted each other, then spread out on the top of the wide hill, setting up their own personal telescopes.

Katrina took a sip of her cocoa. Patrick had made it extra strong and was the perfect contrast to the air that was getting cooler by the second. From this vantage point, the light pollution was minimal, and only a sliver of the moon shone down upon them. The stars twinkled in the distance.

After finishing her cup, she sat it down and listened to the crickets chirping in the grass beside their blanket. It was so peaceful here, so calming after a busy day. A chill ran down Katrina's back as the cool night air made Katrina wrap her arms around herself.

Patrick must have noticed because he set down his own empty cup and gently wrapped an arm around her. "Come here. I'll keep you warm."

She snuggled against his side, and he leaned his head down toward hers as he pointed up at the stars. "Do you see those six bright stars that make some sort of polygon and three that stick out? It looks like a clothing hanger to me."

Katrina turned her head toward Patrick, and he turned his head down toward her. She didn't realize their faces were only a few inches apart until now. "I didn't know you were into astronomy. Do you come to these events often?"

Shaking his head, Patrick said, "No, I admit I've never been to one of these before. Right now, I feel like the ultimate amateur of this amateur astronomy club because I didn't bring along a telescope."

Smiling, Katrina said, "You're no amateur. I just saw you spot that hanger in the sky like a pro, despite not having a telescope. What are those stars supposed to be, anyway? The royal hanger that held the emperor's new clothes? You know, the invisible ones."

Patrick chuckled but didn't move away. "I can't identify any other constellations other than the big dipper, but that one I looked up just for you. That's Leo, the big cat of the sky."

She tilted her head upwards and smiled as she said, "Patrick, that's so sweet. You found a cat in the sky just for me."

Before she knew what happened, Patrick leaned down the last inch and gently pressed his lips against hers. This was no friendly kiss. His lips were soft, and they caused every nerve ending on her own lips to activate. When she didn't respond immediately because of her surprise, he paused and pulled back, but Katrina didn't let him.

She kissed him back and sat up so that she could wrap her arms around his neck. Then she let her lips take control as they pressed against Patrick's with such force and intensity that the eagerness she felt building inside of herself surprised her. Their friendship was already forever changed, but right now, Katrina didn't care.

Patrick used his hand to move her red hair away from her face and cupped her cheek as he pulled her to him with his other arm while he gently brushed the edge of her lips with his tongue. As his one arm wrapped around her small waist, Katrina realized just how muscular he really was. She ran her hand down his bicep and a small appreciative moan escaped her lips unbidden.

No longer shy, Patrick must have heard her moan. His tongue flicked across her own before thrusting into her mouth. Their kisses picked up in intensity, and Katrina grasped his arm and held on as heat flushed through her entire being. She heard a small whine of disappointment escape her own lips as Patrick temporarily pulled away for a breath.

Patrick's fervent lips were back only a moment later, but the reprieve gave Katrina enough mental faculties back to remember where they were. While they had some privacy, they weren't the only ones out here. They were both breathing heavily as she pulled back.

Katrina stared at him, speechless. Her heart beat quickly as her lips yearned to kiss him again. To be in his arms as he kissed her back. He was her best friend, and she spent so much time with him. How did she not realize how manly he was? *All that kayaking must have paid off.*

Patrick's voice was deep and smooth as he spoke. She could just make out his wide eyes in front of her that seemed to beg her for understanding. "Katrina, I need to tell you something. I don't want to be friends anymore."

What in the world does that mean? Was that some kind of passionate goodbye kiss? Did he regret it? Maybe she was enjoying herself too much. Eyebrows raising, she argued, "But, Patrick..."

Patrick cut her off, "I'm not trying to say I don't want you in my life, but the opposite. There is more I need. I can't stand by being your friend while you date other guys and I try to smile like it's all right. I want to be with you. Honestly, Katrina, I need to be with you."

Katrina stared at him, dumbfounded, expecting a night of cocoa and stars, not passionate kisses in the dim moonlight. She stared at Patrick for the first time, not as her best friend but as a man. A nice, thoughtful, handsome, muscular man that she would be crazy not to be head over heels for. Was he the one she wanted?

Speaking more softly, Patrick stared deeply into her eyes, as if trying to read her thoughts. "The truth is, I'm in love with you, Katrina. I have been for a while."

He stared at her, waiting for a response, but for once, Katrina was speechless. Thoughts and emotions rolled through her mind. If they dated and things went wrong, she would not only lose a boyfriend, but her best friend, too. Whose shoulder would be there for her to cry on then? She was kind of afraid that it was too late to go back to just being friends, anyway.

At that moment, only one thing was simple. Only one thing made sense. She really wanted to kiss him again. Katrina leaned forward and kissed him with all the newfound passion that had built up between them. He had to put an arm down to his side to balance himself as she explored his lips. She let go of all the pent-up emotions and confusion and just enjoyed being with him at that moment.

He didn't seem to mind that she didn't answer him with words.

Chapter Thirty-Nine

Epilogue: An American Werewolf in London

Katrina sang one of her favorite songs to herself, *Werewolves of London*, as she walked through her apartment door. She and Patrick were officially dating, and he was coming over this evening for a cuddle and a movie date. Maybe they should watch *An American Werewolf in London*? That was one of her favorites.

She walked up to the door, and it surprised her to see a large package sitting outside of it. There was no delivery label, and the plain brown packing paper didn't show who it was from or where it was going. It was easily ten feet tall by ten feet wide, but only about an inch and a half thick. She unlocked her apartment door and picked it up. While it was tricky to get through the doorway, at least it was light.

She leaned the mysterious package against the inside of the door and bent down to greet the two cats that rubbed against her ankles. "How are my babies doing today? It looks like we got a package. What do you two think it is? Do you think Patrick decided you needed a new giant cat bed? I can't imagine what could be in there. Maybe it isn't for us at all and someone dropped it at the wrong door."

Willa meowed and walked over to her food dish, staring at it without blinking. "All right, all right. I get the point. You couldn't care less what is in this package. You want me to get my priorities straight and feed you first, then figure out this mysterious package later. I'm coming."

After pouring food for both Willa and Captain Jackie, the two cats munched contentedly, oblivious to what she was doing. Maybe that would make it easier, not having to trip over two curious cats while she struggled with this awkwardly large package.

By this point, Katrina was dying of curiosity to find out what was in the package, but she didn't want to rip all the paper off of it if it didn't belong to her. Carefully, she pulled away a single corner of the paper. It was a canvas. That meant one thing, Jared.

She pulled the rest of the paper away swiftly, making sure to not rip the painting. When most of the paper was free, she stood back and gasped. It was the painting Katrina saw at Jared's studio of Willa, but it wasn't the same.

Where before, simple black geometric shapes gave a vague impression of a cat. She could spot the same shapes as the base of the painting, but now shades of every color came together in thick globs to look like Willa's stray scraggly hairs. Instead of trying to smooth out the quirkiness of her cat, this painting celebrated it with vibrant colors.

The painting even captured the essence of Willa's personality with her head cocked and one ear crooked. This was truly a masterpiece that sang to her soul. Wherever he was, Jared had found his voice, and it was a sight to behold.

Katrina looked over every inch of the painting, including the back of the canvas. She saw nothing out of the ordinary. No note. No secret messages, and it didn't even appear to be signed. She would have had no way of knowing it came from Jared if she hadn't seen it in his studio.

Katrina gave a loud sigh as she forced herself to dig for a business card from the FBI out of her wallet. She really hoped they would let her keep the painting after they were done examining it. On the wall behind her couch, there weren't any cat shelves. That would be the perfect place to hang it.

She should probably call Patrick and postpone date night, too. She was sure that after she called the FBI, they would swarm all over her for a few hours. At least it would give her neighbor, Mrs. Danglehauser, something new to gossip about.

Before she dialed, Katrina stood back and took a picture of the painting with her phone, just in case it got confiscated. This was so perfect; she just couldn't bear the thought of parting with it. Then she set Willa in front of the painting. Willa looked up at her, cocking her head, and narrowing one of her eyes in an almost human expression. She snapped the picture, seeing her cat's expression mirrored in the painting.

Staring at the painting, her fingers itched to post it on the Loves Cats forum. She knew she shouldn't, but what if she just shared it with a few of Willa's closest fans? This amazing painting was just too poignant to be locked down in the back of some facility gathering dust. It was meant to be shared. It wouldn't hurt if fewer than a dozen people saw it, right?

She quickly posted the picture to the Loves Cats forum, making sure to only share it with a few select people. She was dying to make sure everyone in her whole cat community saw this amazing art, but privately congratulated herself on her restraint. If the FBI made her hand it over, she could also take down the photo, but it was better to ask for forgiveness, right? Besides, what could it really harm?

She called the department phone number on the card in her hand. A cheery female voice answered. "Hello, operator. How may I direct your call?"

"Yes, I need to talk to Special Agent Daniels." Katrina's phone pinged every few seconds.

The secretary paused. "Can I have a callback number? There is some interference with our call, and I am having a hard time hearing you over all the noise."

After Katrina hung up, she logged back onto the Loves Cat's forum. Some people she'd shared the photo with had shared Willa's portrait. After only a few minutes, the photo already had over a hundred comments and was being shared outside of the group as well. To her surprise, Willa's photo of her with her painting was going viral like nothing Katrina had posted before. It was going wild, and Katrina didn't know how to contain it.

Uh-oh.

The End.

Follow Katrina and Willa as they get mixed up in an art theft mystery!

You can find book 2 in the Loves Cats Series, *Swipe Right for More Cats*, in Cozy Adventure Club: https://reamstories.com/miranda-herald

Did you enjoy this story?

I would really appreciate your help by leaving a short, honest review in your favorite store. This not only helps me to gain visibility of my stories, but helps other readers find a good book that they would enjoy. Thank you in advance and happy reading!

10 Prequel Scenes from the Loves Cats Series

Excerpt from Willa's Blooper Reel

Katrina sorted all the fresh flowers into piles around her living room. *This smells wonderful. I hope they keep this powerful scent for the shower tomorrow.* She sat down in the only open space left on the floor and looked around her.

She had twenty-three flower centerpieces to finish by tomorrow. They were going to meet at eight in the morning to set up the hall for her sister, Susan's bridal shower. *I wish I had an easier time at work today. I was hoping to be fresher before tackling this.*

I'm just swamped at work right now. We had a lot of new cats come in recently. Last week, one of my volunteers told me they got a new job, and she doesn't have the time to help anymore. Another told me today that they were moving. It looks like I will be recruiting new volunteers next week.

Katrina picked up one of the glass vases and groaned. *This is going to take me all night, but what choice do I have? I guess I will have to stay up as late as it takes to finish this project.* She turned on the television in the background and filled the bottom of the vases with glass beads.

Willa sat napping behind her on the couch while she fiddled around with the flowers. Katrina tried a few different arrangements until she got the perfect look. She fiddled around with tying a perfect bow from the coordinating ribbon and then snapped a picture to send to her sister.

Good. One arrangement done, twenty-two to go. At my current rate of one flower arrangement per every half hour, that's only eleven more hours to go. Katrina put her head in her hands. *What have I gotten myself into?*

Katrina got to work. At one point, Willa came over and sat on top of a pile of flowers. "No, no, Willa. Come on. You can't sit there. You'll smash them. Here, it's almost dinnertime. Why don't I get you some food?" Katrina got up and poured cat food into Willa's dish. Willa munched happily as Katrina went back to work.

Luckily, now that she got the design down, she pumped out eight more arrangements over the next two hours. Katrina was midway through the next one when she decided that she really needed a break. She stood up, stretched her legs, and made some tea.

When she got back into the living room, she sat back down in front of her partially finished arrangement. *I thought I already put a purple one in there.* She picked up a new purple one. *I guess I didn't. The flowers are already running together.*

Katrina had twelve arrangements complete when she noticed that there were half as many of the yellow flowers as the pink and purple ones. *Oh no. The florist must have miscounted. I don't have enough yellow. What can I do? Maybe if we use the ones with yellow flowers on every other table, it won't be a big deal that some have yellow and some don't.*

She tried out arranging a centerpiece with no yellow flowers and added extra baby's breath so that they still looked full and put it beside the completed arrangements that had yellow. *I like it. Instead of being overwhelmed with yellow, it gives more of a hint of yellow.* Convinced it solved the problem, Katrina continued on.

Around two in the morning, Katrina was down to her last two arrangements. She was growing cross-eyed and developed a weird aversion to pink, purple, and yellow flowers. She reached for a flower to her side, when she realized that there were none of the pink flowers left.

Katrina became suspicious and looked around. *It's one thing if the florist miscounted the yellow flowers, but I recounted the pink and purple ones only a few hours ago. The only one other living thing in the house was... Willa.*

Katrina turned around to see Willa innocently sitting on the couch behind her. Unfortunately, the thief made a mistake. Upon closer inspection, she saw a yellow flower petal in her fur. Exhausted, she sternly asked, "Willa, what have you been doing with my flowers?"

Willa continued to look on, completely innocent. Katrina pretended like she was back at work, making another flower arrangement, while carefully watching the remaining purple flowers.

Out of the corner of her eye, she watched Willa silently pad over to the flower pile. She picked a flower up in her jaws and traveled behind the couch to sneak it out of the room, unseen. Katrina stood up slowly to see where she was taking the flower.

Willa turned the corner into her bedroom and climbed under the bed. There she laid her latest acquisition on-top of a nest of flowers she made. Immediately, she rolled all over them, crumpling the new flower to match the other ruined flowers.

Katrina felt like she could cry. *I worked so hard on these arrangements all night. I'm so close to finishing. Where am I going to get more fresh flowers at this time of night?* She gently scolded Willa for taking things that weren't hers. Willa lowered her head and slunk further under the bed, knowing she was caught.

Katrina picked up the scattered pieces of flowers. *There's no salvaging these. I simply don't have time to go pick up new flowers tomorrow morning. These last two centerpieces were for the head table. I can't just set them up there with a few purple flowers and some leftover baby's breath flowers.*

Willa looked out under the bed and softly meowed. A cranky Katrina scowled. "Maybe I should put you in one of the centerpieces. At least then it would look full. Then Susan could bring her cat, Biscuit, to put in the second one. It would look perfectly full and balanced." The offhanded comment sparked an idea in Katrina's mind.

The next morning, Susan gushed over the flower arrangements. "I can't believe you finished these all yourself! They turned out beautiful and smell great too."

A bit about Miranda Herald

Typing by moonlight and powered by tea, I love reading and writing whenever I can fit it in. I find a good mind boggling puzzle or escape room exhilarating and was excited to include them in my latest works. I hope you enjoy my puzzling twist on romance and join my characters for many more adventures!

I love to hear from my readers and want you to join my community on Facebook, Tiktok, and Instagram. Check out my website to find all of my freebies, novels, and social links. You can find everything at my website **www.mirandaherald.com.**

Join my membership community for pre-release books and exclusive exclusive content!

https://reamstories.com/page/mirandaherald

What happens in Adventure Club stays in Adventure Club

I have an amazing opportunity for my readers- Join Cozy Adventure Club!

Members can receive:

Early access: Read my current work in progress earlier than on serial platforms and have access to the full book before it officially launches.

Library access: Read ALL of my previous books for one low price!

Cozy book club: Discuss your cozy reads and all the good feels with the author and other like-minded community members.

Exclusive bonus content: Get interviews with characters, deleted scenes, games, and more.

Sneak Peeks: Be one of the few with behind the scenes information. See cover art as its being created and learn the next book I'm writing before anyone else.

Come for the cozy adventures and stay for the memorable quirky characters.

Join my membership community for pre-release books and exclusive content!

https://reamstories.com/mirandaherald

Printed in the USA
CPSIA information can be obtained
at www.ICGtesting.com
LVHW041618290923
759456LV00004B/119

9 798987 251539